Critical acclaim for Robert Barnard:

'One of our most original and versatile bloodspillers'
Marcel Berlins, The Times

'He plots a mystery as well as any other writer alive, and
he never takes the easy path of repeating a winning formula'
Time Magazine

'Offers what Christie could not: wit . . . and a sense of
energy and style'
Newsweek

'He can write most under the table with one hand tied
behind his back'
T.J. Binyon, The Times Literary Supplement

Also by Robert Barnard

BODIES
THE DISPOSAL OF THE LIVING
POLITICAL SUICIDE
OUT OF THE BLACKOUT

and published by Corgi Books

SHEER TORTURE

Robert Barnard

CORGI BOOKS

SHEER TORTURE

A CORGI BOOK   0 552 13372 8

Originally published in Great Britain by
William Collins Sons & Co. Ltd

PRINTING HISTORY
William Collins edition published 1981
Corgi edition published 1989

This book is set in 10/11pt Plantin.

Corgi Books are published by Transworld Publishers Ltd.,
61-63 Uxbridge Road, Ealing, London W5 5SA, in Australia by
Transworld Publishers (Australia) Pty. Ltd., 15-23 Helles
Avenue, Moorebank, NSW 2170, and in New Zealand by Transworld
Publishers (N.Z.) Ltd., Cnr. Moselle and Waipareira Avenues,
Henderson, Auckland.

Printed and bound in Great Britain by
Cox & Wyman Ltd, Reading

CONTENTS

CHAPTER 1

OBITUARY

I first heard of the death of my father when I saw his obituary in *The Times*. I skimmed through it, cast my eye over the Court Circular, and was about to turn to the leader page when I was struck by something odd in the obituary and went back to it.

'As reported on page 3, the death has occurred . . .' was how it began. That was odd. Famous actresses, disgraced politicians, exploded royalty might get their deaths reported on the news pages, but why should my father? Even the obituary had admitted that his achievements were few – had implied, indeed, that had he not been a member of a family whose fame verged on notoriety they would hardly have paid him the compliment of an obituary at all. 'Though now rarely heard, his song-cycle *Dolores* . . .' – that kind of thing. My father's death would shatter the world no more than it had shattered me. And in that case there must be something unusual about the death – a spectacular accident, suicide (no, not that), or . . .

Going against all my principles (for like all right-thinking people I read my paper backwards) I turned to page three. And there it was, tucked away down at the bottom: 'Police were called to Harpenden House late last night after the death was reported of Leo Trethowan, youngest member of the famous Trethowan family . . .' Well, well: so the old boy had gone out with a bang.

I turned back to the centre pages, but I found it hard to concentrate on the first leader (which was about changes in the Anglican liturgy, never a subject of urgent personal interest to me). In spite of myself, in spite of the affectation of total indifference which I assumed even when alone, it had to be admitted that I was interested. My mind was already toying with various enticing speculations: a spectacular accident was of course a possibility, but it seemed to me that, knowing my father, it was odds on he had met his unexpected death at the hands of someone or other. Certainly he would not have committed suicide: he was never one to do anybody a favour. No, on the whole murder seemed . . .

It was then that the telephone rang.

'Perry Trethowan,' I said.

'Hello, Perry,' said my superior at the other end. 'Have you read the paper yet?'

'Yes,' I said cautiously. 'The Common Market summit seems to be sticky going.'

There was a second's pause. I have a nasty vein of dry facetiousness that a lot of people find trying, and my boss was one of them. He was trying to decide whether it was operational now. 'I was referring to the death of your father,' he said cautiously.

'Oh yes, I saw that.'

'But of course, they must have telegrammed you last night anyway.'

'No.'

'You'll be going down for the funeral, I take it?'

'I hadn't thought to,' I said. 'I wouldn't be expected.'

'Isn't this a time to let bygones be bygones?'

'That's what I try to do. I finished with my family years ago.'

'Perry, you're being difficult. You know we've been called in?'

I pricked up my ears. 'Ah. So it was murder?'

'Yes, it was. Almost definitely. Of course there's no question of sending you down—'

'No, thank God,' I said. 'Who are you sending?'

'Hamnet. What's your opinion of him?'

'Perfectly decent chap. Excellent choice.'

'It just seemed to me that perhaps he's a bit lacking in
. . . well, imagination. And with your family imagination
might be exactly what is wanted.'

'Personally I'd have said a thoroughly nasty mind was the
first requisite for anyone investigating the murder of a
Trethowan,' I said incautiously, giving him an opening.

'Well, you should know. That's really why we'd like to
have you down there—'

'I do not have a nasty mind.'

'But you do know all the inside secrets. You are on their
wavelength. Of course, I'd heard you weren't close . . .'

I laughed. 'A nice way of putting it.'

'Do you have any financial interest in the death, may
I ask?'

'Certainly not. I was cut off without a penny. If there is
anything much to inherit (which I wouldn't bank on) it will
go to my sister, which is quite as it should be: she is precisely
the sort of person odd legacies do go to.'

'He could have changed his mind, of course.'

'My father never, but never, changed his mind.'

'Well, that's all to the good as far as we're concerned.'

'Thank you.'

'I mean if you have as little as possible personal interest
in the matter.'

'Joe,' I said, addressing the Deputy Assistant Commissioner in a way I would usually not do except over an off-
duty pint, 'we are both agreed, aren't we, that I cannot have
any part in the investigation of this murder? I can brief
Hamnet, I can even put in an appearance for a couple of
hours at the funeral. But surely nothing more can be asked
of me than that?'

'I thought,' said Joe Grierly, 'that since you could be
down there for perfectly natural reasons over the next few
days, you could be given something in the nature of a
watching brief. There are features in this case . . .'

I groaned audibly. 'There would be features,' I said.

'The personalities involved, for example, present problems:

I don't know whether you knew, but one of your father's sisters – Catherine, I think the name is – went off her head last year.'

'How did they know?' I asked.

'Eh?'

'My Aunt Kate has been teetering on the edge of insanity for fifty years. One would hardly notice when she actually toppled over.'

'Wasn't there something about the war?' Joe asked, cunningly vague.

'My aunt had various mad crushes in her teens, on people like Isadora Duncan and D. H. Lawrence, and she capped them by becoming a besotted admirer of Adolf Hitler. She used to spend her summers attending Nuremberg rallies and consorting with Hitler's *Mädchen* in Bavarian work camps – some sort of Butlins plus ideology, I gather. They interned her in Holloway during the war.'

'Oh I say – that seems rather hard.'

'Not a bit: I've every sympathy with the authorities. If the silly . . . buzzard had kept quiet everything would have been forgotten. Instead of which she went careering round the village on her bike distributing pamphlets calling for a German victory. They really had no option. She had a highly privileged life in Holloway with others of like mind. As far as I can gather they all sat around complaining about the quality of the port.'

'Poor old thing.'

'She was thirty or so at the time,' I pointed out.

'I can see I'm not going to rouse any sympathy in you for the difficult position your family's in at the moment.'

'No.'

'How did you and your father come to disagree?'

'We never agreed. How did we come to fight? Well, you know how in the past families like ours expected their sons to go into the army, the church, manage the estate and so on, and there was a great stink if one of them wanted to go on the stage or something?'

10

'Yes.'

'Well, our family's cussed in this as in everything else. If I'd said I wanted to go to ballet school, or train to be a drop-out, or go to the States and graduate in dope-peddling, they'd probably have patted me on the head and given me the family blessing and a couple of thou. When I said I wanted to join the army, all hell broke loose. My father said it was a pathetically conformist way of life, Aunt Sybilla said it showed a dreadfully coarse nature, and Aunt Kate said I'd be *on the wrong side.*'

'It was no better when you switched to the police?'

'I didn't enquire. But I assure you, no – no, they would *not* have looked more favourably on the police.'

'Your Aunt Sybilla, she's some sort of artist, isn't she?'

'My Aunt Sybilla is or was a stage designer; my Uncle Lawrence is a poet and writer of *belles lettres* sort of stuff; my father was a composer and my Aunt Kate is – well, I suppose you could call her a politician.'

'Well, you see the problems Hamnet is going to face when he gets down there.'

'My sympathy goes out to him,' I said.

'Look, Perry, it'll be much the best thing for all of us if you go into this voluntarily. After all, they are your family. Blood is thicker than water.'

'So my professional experience tells me,' I said. 'Personally, taking it metaphorically, I've never been able to extract much meaning from that saw. Blood is certainly *stickier* than water – that I do know.'

'Christ, I don't want to have to *draft* you—'

'Oh, hell's bells, all right. I'll go down for the funeral.'

'You'll go down today. And you'll stay down there as long as Hamnet needs you.'

'No wonder men are resigning from the Force in droves,' I said. 'This is nothing but jackboot tyranny.'

'Have fun,' said Joe, registering my surrender.

I was just banging down the phone when I remembered something I'd forgotten to ask. 'Here, Joe,' I shouted, 'you haven't told me how he died.'

11

Joe obviously resumed the conversation with reluctance. 'I was afraid you'd ask that,' he said.

'Not nice?' I asked, now really curious.

'He died,' said Joe cautiously, 'while subjecting himself to a form of torture which I believe is called strappado.'

'Oh, no!' I howled.

'He had it arranged, I gather, so that he could stop it at will. As far as we can see, someone fiddled with the ropes.'

'Joe, listen,' I gabbled, 'you can't send me to that snake pit. That is *just* how one of my family would die, and *just* how one of my family would murder. This is appalling. The press will have a field day. I'll be the laughing-stock of the CID for the rest of my life. You can't send me there, Joe—'

'There's a train at ten fifty,' said the Deputy Assistant Commissioner. 'Oh, and there's one more tiny detail—'

'What?'

'He was wearing gauzy spangled tights at the time.'

CHAPTER 2

HOMECOMING

The inconvenient, and slightly ludicrous, house which my great-grandfather finished building in the last years of the Old Queen's reign must, over the years, have brought a small fortune to British Rail and its predecessor companies from successive generations of my family, and in its heyday, their numerous guests. Perhaps this was why the Beeching axe quivered with compunction in the early 'sixties and spared the nearest station of Thornwick, and why subsequent carve-ups of the public transport system designed to force more and more cars out on to the roads have left it standing and (with reduced services) functioning. It's not every day you meet a large family of lunatics ready to travel from Northumberland to London at the drop of a hat.

Not, I suppose, that the state of the family finances, or the state of the family limbs come to that, encourages that sort of genteel hoboism nowadays.

Anyway, I caught the ten fifty Edinburgh train (because, when all is said and done, you may wrangle and grumble, wriggle and chafe with your superiors in the Force, but you don't disobey their orders) and after changing trains at Newcastle I chugged into Thornwick some time around four. I was oddly touched when the stationmaster, after all these years, said 'Sad business, Mr Peregrine' as he took my ticket, though no one had used the appalling full form of my Christian name with my permission for years.

When, twenty minutes later, my taxi swung through the gates of Harpenden House and up the curved approach, I was cured of any lump-in-the-throat nostalgia by the sight of the house itself. (You are getting all this stuff about trains and stationmasters and ancestral piles because I don't think you're strong enough yet to meet the Trethowan family *en masse*. Did you think you'd heard all there was to hear about them in the first chapter? Oh no, dear reader: you haven't heard the half of it yet.)

The house, Harpenden, has just nothing to recommend it – except its size, and even that is more than a trifle ridiculous. My great-grandfather had few qualities to plead his case at the Judgment Seat except a very great deal of money, but even a filthy rich Victorian was expected to build with a modicum of discretion. Pevsner, who is searingly honest about the building, names the architects as 'Hubert Selby-Grossmith, succeeded at a late stage in the enterprise by Auberon Biggsworth,' and he might have added that my great-grandfather aided, abetted and tyrannized over the enterprise from beginning to end, having the infernal good fortune to die between completion and moving-in day. The architects, chivvied, bullied and finally swapped midstream, were told to impose the Trethowans on Northumberland: they did so in the form (roughly) of an enormous lowish central block with four turretty wings at each corner. Does that sound regular and sane to you? Well, I should add that each wing is a fantasy based on a different style and period of architecture, that the massive central block acquired certain accretions, that . . .

In fact, even John Betjeman, faced with it on arrival for a house party in the early 'thirties, could only stutter 'It's jolly . . . jolly *arresting.*' And when he tried to write an impromptu verse about it during his visit, the future Laureate's feet moved in classical metres, and the result was so lugubrious it has appeared in none of his collections. The house has affected most of its visitors in pretty much the same way. It depresses me no end, even now, and as we drove up the sudden swerve in the drive which led to the front door (the result of a last-minute geriatric whim of my great-grandfather's) and I was disgorged on to the

14

main steps, I fancied that the taxi-driver shook his head in sympathy. Or perhaps he had heard about the death. Or had driven some of the inhabitants.

It seemed funny to ring, but ring I did. The taxi sat there, the driver separating his tip from his fare, unnecessarily slowly, I thought, and I wondered whether he knew who I was and was interested to see my reception. Was this the beginning of the hideous general public interest that I had foreseen? Eventually the door opened on a smallish, sandy-haired manservant with a manner that (perhaps assumed temporarily) seemed set to repel invaders.

'Good afternoon,' I said, feeling slightly ridiculous. 'I'm Perry Trethowan . . . Mr Leo Trethowan's son.'

His face changed, but only to cautious welcome. 'Oh, Mr Peregrine.' (His voice was gentle, Lowland Scots, and made a meal of the r's in Peregrine.) 'Won't you come in, sir?' Once in the hall he turned on the soft sympathy. 'A terrible business, sir. You have my wife's and my sympathy, indeed you do. Would you . . . would you wait while I inform Miss Sybilla . . . and Sir Lawrence?'

And without waiting for an answer he left me in the hall, while he made off in the direction of the main drawing-room. I reflected on the order of the names: would it not have been natural to mention my Uncle Lawrence first? I stood there, looking around the entrance hall, four times the size of a family council flat, its ceiling five times a man's height, looming in some brown cobwebby heaven up there. It was exactly as I remembered it – its gloom, its stuffed heads of animals slaughtered for the size of their antlers, its monstrously large picture of my great-grandfather, executed (the picture, I mean) by Sir Harold Hardacre, RA, in 1887. Many painters of the period have long ago recovered from the rock-bottom prices they fetched in the 'twenties, but my great-grandfather selected, to commit him to posterity, artists whom no amount of recovered piety could render desirable. One had the impression that he paid them by the square yard.

Nevertheless, since the little Scotsman did not return, I

went to the far wall to gaze irreverently on my great-grandsire. He had been, like me, a large man, and the size therefore had a certain appropriateness. Mill- and mine-owner, captain of industry, were written on his face. He had been as well in his time a 'useful public figure,' and that was there too. Believing in the untrammelled freedom of Capital, in the absolute right of men such as himself to pay their men as little as possible and to take no thought whatsoever to their safety at work, he had naturally entered Parliament as a Radical. In the course of time he had become an orthodox Liberal; then he had split with his leader over Home Rule and become a Liberal Unionist. It was very easy, then, to move to the Right without giving anyone the opportunity to label you turncoat. He had held minor office in weak governments that needed the broadest possible basis of support, and had been a great trial. Lord Rosebery had called him, under provocation, a pig-headed nincompoop, and in spite of the best efforts of Sir Harold Hardacre, RA, that had got into the picture too.

Still the little Scot did not return. An impossible hope rose in me. Could it be that they were refusing to see me? Was I being barred from the ancestral door? Could I not then return quite justifiably to Scotland Yard and report to Joe the satisfactory failure of my mission? I was just weakly nourishing such hopes when a door softly opened.

'Sir Lawrence is in the drawing-room, Mr Peregrine, with your two aunts,' said the ingratiating voice, 'and they'll be pleased to see you now.'

My heart sank again. 'Thank you – I'm sorry, I don't know your name.'

'McWatters, sir. Shall I take your case to one of the guest-rooms?' He gestured towards the tiny case (suitable for a *very* short stay) which I had set down by the main door.

'No, McWatters, better wait a bit,' I said, ever the optimist. Squaring my shoulders I marched across the vast expanse of hall and into the drawing-room.

My eye was met, first of all and inevitably, by my great-grandfather again, in position over the mantelpiece in the

16

version of himself perpetrated, for just that position, by Sir Richard Fairweather, RA, in 1896 – very much the same as the one in the hall, except that nine more years of pigheadedness and nincompoopery had lined their way on to the face. Around the other walls were large masterpieces I remembered, by Maclise, Frith, Waterhouse and others, as well as newer ones, portraits, by my Aunt Elizabeth, the real artist of the family, who died when I was still a child. Dwarfed by all this oil and varnish, in two uncomfortable armchairs and a wheelchair, were my Aunt Sybilla, my Aunt Kate, and my Uncle Lawrence. Sybilla rose, somewhat unsteady on her pins, to greet me.

'Good afternoon, Peregrine,' she said. 'This is quite a surprise. Oh dear, still so *large*? . . . Even *larger*, I think?' (Six-feet-five, seventeen stone, enthusiastic amateur weightlifter and shot-putter, I could only nod agreement that I was even larger. She shook her head regretfully, as if shrinking would have been the best sign that I repented my odd notions.) 'Your Aunt Kate, your Uncle Lawrence.'

I kissed Aunt Kate, who stood to attention to allow it, and then burst into a disconcerting chuckle of laughter. I had to take Uncle Lawrence by the hand to shake it, since he seemed immobile, but as I did so he shouted, 'Who? Who?', and then seemed to relapse into a doze. To relieve the awkwardness of the situation Sybilla said, 'Would you like some tea?' but she seemed displeased when I accepted. She was forced to ring for McWatters and order tea and, after a pause, sandwiches and cake. The prodigal son, I felt, got a much more wholehearted culinary welcome.

'Er . . . you've come about your poor father, I suppose?' said Sybilla, unusually uncertainly for her, I felt, since she was so seldom less than mistress of any situation.

'Of course he's come about Leo,' bellowed Aunt Kate. 'Don't be a blithering ninny. Give him the details, then! Give him all the details!'

'Kate!' shrilled Sybilla. But Kate's parade-ground tones had unfortunately woken Uncle Lawrence, who immediately started up with his 'Who? Who?' routine again.

'*Peregrine*,' said Aunt Sybilla in her loud, hard tones, like a malignant bell-bird. 'Your nephew Peregrine. Leo's son, you remember.'

'Oh, Leo's son,' nodded the patriarchal head. 'Well, what are you wasting time for? Show him up to Leo!'

At which, mercifully, he nodded off again, and McWatters came in with the tea-things.

Perhaps I should take advantage of the pause to describe the surviving members of my father's generation, grandchildren of the imperious frock-coated numbskull staring down at us in all his eight-feet-high splendour from over the marble fireplace. My Uncle Lawrence's most remarkable physical feature was his shaggy, venerable man-of-letters head: its mane of white hair might have been (in fact, probably was) combed outwards to emphasize its size and distinction, to provide a striking frame for the classic lines of the face, the shaggy moustache, the keen (though now senseless) eyes. Lawrence Trethowan, his appearance proclaimed, was a Literary Man. He had survived the First World War and had written some agonized sonnets on it, much praised by Eddie Marsh and other literary gents of the era. After that (for want of subject matter, I take it) he had declined into writing rather feeble nature lyrics, stuff about country lanes and whatnot, and this was hardly attuned to the public mood. But he had also written occasional essays – 'delightful' was the usual way of describing them – for declining periodicals, and in collected form they entranced the Boots library subscribers of the 'thirties and 'forties. He had been inexplicably knighted in 1964, by which time he was unread if not forgotten (my family, alas, has never been forgotten).

My Aunt Sybilla had aged less gracefully. In her youth she had been known for her spry, sharp, gamine qualities – qualities which easily grow sour with age. She had designed the sets and costumes for that bright young review *Wits!* in 1929, and its nearly as successful successor *Quits!* in 1931 (both revues still affectionately remembered by old ladies in St John's Wood and their older flames in Highgate). She had designed things for Coward (who had seen through her), for the young Rattigan, and had even done a spry, witty *Orfeo* for Sadler's Wells, which nobody who understood the opera had really liked. Her career had collapsed with the war and had never got going after it, though Covent Garden, notoriously prone to pick lame ducks when it comes to designers, did employ her on a couple of misconceived ballets. She was now – and had been as long as I can remember – a vinegary, pretentious bundle of egocentric extravagances, a succession of ghastly, ill-fitting artistic poses. It's living with people like Aunt Sybilla makes a man take up weightlifting.

Aunt Kate, as ever, was square, gruff and ludicrous, but now she had – perhaps regained from her childhood, and the result of last year's breakdown – a dreadfully hockey-stick schoolgirl roguishness peering through the heartiness. I never could actually dislike my Aunt Kate, but she exasperated me thoroughly: plenty of people were silly enough to admire Hitler before 1939, but to persist in that admiration forty years later seemed to call for a superhuman kind of silliness that was all but repellent.

Anyway, there we sat, over tea and cress sandwiches, one big happy family.

Lawrence ate little. He woke, looked at me, muttered 'Oh, yes,' and was handed a cress sandwich, which he wolfed down. Kate handed him another, but after one bite he fell asleep, and she took the rest of it from his hand with surprising gentleness, then went back to stolidly munching her own.

'I apologize for Lawrence,' said Sybilla sharply. 'He is *not* always like this. In fact, this is what Mrs McWatters calls "one of his off days" – which is a very vulgar phrase, but it does rather sum it up, doesn't it?'

I did not respond to this invitation to ridicule my Uncle Lawrence (though only, probably, because it came from my Aunt Sybilla). Aunt Kate, by this time, was positively bouncing with suppressed puppyish enthusiasm.

'*Syb!*' she said. 'You haven't told him. Oh, go on, Syb! Tell him the details!'

I found this – even *I* found this – rather ghoulish. 'I think I know the main outlines.'

'*Really?*' said Sybilla, clearly affronted at being cheated of her story. 'But no. You can't possibly. You can't have talked to Cristobel, and nothing has appeared in the public prints.'

Deliberate archaisms were one of Aunt Sybilla's favourite forms of affectation.

'I'm not dependent entirely on the public prints,' I said. 'I heard it from my superior in the police force.'

'The Po*lice*! Have you joined the Po*lice*? I thought you were in the army! Kate, did we know Peregrine was a Peeler?'

'I knew,' said Kate, chomping vigorously at her sandwich like a young horse. 'I've known for jolly ages!'

'I left the army eight years ago,' I said. 'I went into the police. I'm a detective-inspector with the CID. I expect to be a superintendent before long.'

'Spare me the details of the promotional ladder in the Metropolitan Police Force,' said Aunt Sybilla, flapping an aesthetic claw. But I thought she was interested too, because, nibbling delicately at a piece of seed cake, she said: 'Well, well, so you're in the police. Really, you must forgive me, Perry dear – not knowing, or forgetting. But the fact is, your father did not . . . very frequently . . . *talk* about you, you know!'

'I'm sure he didn't,' I said. 'We each went our own way a long time ago.'

'Yes, indeed – thirteen years, is it? Or fourteen? A long time. And now you'd be – ah, yes, thirty-two. So you heard about our little problem in . . . in the course of duty, as it were?'

It struck me, momentarily, that the Aunts were taking this with a quite chilling degree of calmness. Then I realized that sensation, public clamour, the scorn of *vox populi*, these were meat and drink to a Trethowan: the legend had been a pure publicity creation, and if my father at his death had been recognized as an obscure minor composer, he would have been a totally unknown one had it not been for the Trethowan PR machine. And much the same went for Lawrence and Syb.

'I was officially informed of my father's death,' I said stiffly, 'and of some of the details. You can probably tell me more, I imagine.'

Kate bounced anew. She made an odd, soaring gesture with her hands to signify being hauled up, then, with relish, a great swooping one to signify being dropped down. 'Bump! Ouch!' she guffawed.

'Catherine! Any more and you leave the room!'

'Oh Syb, you are a spoilsport.'

'Your father,' said Sybilla gravely, turning to me (but I thought I detected a certain enjoyment in her, too), 'met his end while conducting one of his little experiments. Of course, you know all about them . . .'

'To be frank, Aunt Sybilla, I don't. You forget the last time I saw him I was only eighteen. I had some . . . inkling . . . about his tastes. But the fact is, I really don't think he was actually . . . experimenting, at that time.'

She thought, her scratchy little face, all crow's-feet and old chicken skin, puckered in malicious calculation.

'You know, I think you must be right. The experiments came later, I think. With age. Probably he needed more . . . stimulation. Anyway, the fact is, Peregrine, your father was exceedingly interested in the tortures of the Spanish Inquisition (among others), and he began to experiment to see whether he might not . . . reproduce their effects . . . if you understand me . . . on himself.'

At this point Aunt Kate could not repress another chortle.

'I see. Now, was this something that was generally known – I mean in this house?'

'Oh, yes. We're a very unconventional family, as you know, Peregrine. We are not censorious: we can encompass human variety. No, give your father his due: he wasn't like those poor little men who shop furtively in Soho. He never made a grubby little secret of it!'

21

I was seized with a conviction that the best thing to do, if you have inclinations like my father's, was to make a grubby little secret of the fact.

'When you say you all knew,' I said, trying not to make this sound like a police enquiry and not succeeding very well, 'what does that mean? Did he invite you all to exhibition performances?'

'You are being a teeny bit vulgar, Peregrine dear. No, he did not. Though I'm quite sure he would not have minded. I would not have thought twice of breaking in on him, if anything important had come up. He talked about it quite openly, even at meals.'

'I watched him through the keyhole once,' volunteered Aunt Kate. She was going to do a repetition of her pantomime, but thought better of it.

'I see,' I said. 'So the whole household would have known. And so what happened?'

'Well, of course, it was just a *little* unwise, at his age. And I suppose he overdid it . . .' She averted her eyes. 'They say a thread snapped, or a pulley broke, or something, and he just . . . couldn't stop it.'

'I see.'

'That's really all there is. Your poor sister—' she looked at me conspiratorially, to see whether we mightn't have a snigger together over my poor sister, but I maintained my professional policeman's poker face — 'your poor sister woke towards midnight, wanted some water or something; she heard the machine still going, and she went down and . . . found him, poor thing. She had hysterics all over the house. And it's a big house to have hysterics all over.'

'Poor Cristobel,' I said. 'And at the moment the police are in possession of father's wing, I take it.'

'Exactly. Though why they should have been called I don't know. Anyway, they're infesting the entire house.' A thought transparently crossed her face, and she leaned towards me. 'Now, Peregrine, dear boy, let me have your candid opinion. What is the best thing for us to do?'

In a flash I understood that Aunt Syb was on the horns

of a dilemma. On the one hand there was the aristocratic (well, upper-middle, with oodles of the necessary) instinct, bred into her, that at times of family crises one sat tight, closed ranks, said nothing, and waited for things to die down. On the other hand there was the newer Trethowan feeling (fostered by her and her siblings) that everything ought to be capitalized on, everything done to the clashing cymbals of publicity. The Trethowan legend, the creation of publicity, had been kept alive by periodic injections of it (including one hideously embarrassing libel action I remember from my adolescence). Now my father's death could perhaps be the latest in a long line of front-page spreads. She rather nauseated me, did my Aunt Syb.

'Well,' I said, cautiously and reluctantly, 'the first thing to say is that, even if it was an accident, it can't – the strappado business and so on – be kept quiet. There will have to be a coroner's inquest—'

At this point my Aunt Kate clapped her hands with happy anticipation and woke Uncle Lawrence, who began to shout: 'What am I doing here? Gross negligence on somebody's part! Why haven't I been put to bed?'

'Take him up, Kate,' said Sybilla. 'No, this minute! You brought it on yourself!' And Kate, dragging her old feet, began the long wheeling of Lawrence's chair towards the door. I rose to help her, but Sybilla's arm restrained me.

'No. It does her good. Gives her something to think about. You know she was Not Well last year?'

'I heard she had some kind of . . . breakdown,' I ventured.

'All that *wonderful* strength of mind – gone! As you can see. Now, you say there is no chance at all of keeping all this *absolutely* quiet?'

'None at all, I'm afraid.'

'Well, then, we'll have to make the most of it,' said Aunt Sybilla, with something like a happy smile on her face.

'I don't quite know what you mean by that, Aunt Sybilla, but . . .'

'Now never you mind, Peregrine. You leave this to me. I *know* the press! I've been dealing with them for years!

Meanwhile *you* — since you are here, by happy chance — can help me by being my *liaison* with the gentlemen of the Police! You must know this man they've sent. Get in with him! Find out what he's up to! And I can feed judicious fragments of information to my friends. Oh, by the way, you will stay for the funeral, won't you?'

'I—'

'Then that's settled. I'll go and tell McWatters to get a spare room ready. Your father's wing—?'

'Well, there are places I'd rather—'

'Splendid, that's settled. And I'll tell Mrs McWatters there'll be one extra for dinner. I'll try and get *all* the family there for dinner, a real reunion. That will be nice, won't it?'

'Yes, well, perhaps I'd better go and see Superintendent Hamnet.'

'No hurry, Peregrine dear. Do finish those sandwiches. You look as if you need an . . . awful *lot* of food.'

And she tottered out with the tinkling laugh that had echoed through the smaller London theatres on dress-rehearsal days in the 'thirties. I took another sandwich and was just stuffing it into my mouth (to get a healthy sized bite) when she surprised me by putting her birdlike head around the door again.

'Oh, by the way, are you married, Peregrine?'

'Yes, I am actually. But—'

'Splendid. Thought I ought to know. I didn't want to make another *false step* — like about the police. Do gobble up all those, won't you? Dinner's not until eight thirty.'

I cursed her, but I did as I was told. I took the plate and stood with it in the centre of that enormous room. Chomping away, with Trethowanian irreverence, I gazed at the portrait of my great-grandfather. I winked at it, but it was one of those portraits that could never, by any stretch of the imagination, seem to wink back. I looked at the enormous, wonderfully literal Victorian story-telling canvases: *The Love Potion*; *The Capulets' Ball*; *Bank Holiday on Hampstead Heath*. They had been on the family walls over a period so long that their critical esteem must have

24

done a graph rather like a political party's between general elections.

Then I looked at the portraits – by my dead aunt, Elizabeth Trethowan. The witty, affectionate one of her father (my grandfather, the first actual occupant of this elephantine monstrosity of a house). Then the little group of pictures of her brothers and sisters, done just after the war: Lawrence, posing like mad as the Man of Letters; Kate – stern in greens and khakis; my father, looking every inch a minor composer. And my eye came to rest on the picture of Sybilla – all bright modern blues, greys and pinks, colours which highlighted the crow's feet around the eyes, the discontented droop of the mouth, the souring of the bright little talent of ten or fifteen years earlier.

I have always said that Aunt Eliza was the only one of the family with talent. I'd go further: there was a touch of genius about the work of Aunt Eliza at her peak. And she was dead these twenty years or more, leaving behind the brood of siblings that had swung merrily into the glare of publicity on the skirt-tails of her gifts. 'That enormously vital and gifted family', *The Times* had generously called them. Us. No, it was wrong. There was really only one Trethowan.

CHAPTER 3

THE PAINFUL DETAILS

Eventually it had to be faced up to. I supposed that Hamnet was still at work in my father's wing of the house, and before dinner I would have to meet and face the appalling *professional* embarrassment of my father's death.

I left the drawing-room, crossing the gargantuan hall on my way to the Gothic wing where my father and sister, and myself when young, had had their home. But as I passed through the hall my eye was caught by a lectern standing near the door, on which was placed an enormous book well remembered from my childhood: Great-Grandfather Trethowan's Family Bible. It had always stood, before, in the chapel – now, I presumed, not merely disused but abandoned. I went over and opened it, curiously, for here were entered all the family births, marriages and deaths – things Hamnet would no doubt expect me to have at my fingertips, though in fact of all that had happened in the family over the past thirteen years or so I had merely the haziest of notions, culled from occasional meetings with my sister, or the inevitable newspaper paragraphs.

So here (in thick black Gothic script) they all were: on the first page JOSIAH BENTHAM TRETHOWAN, 1828-97; his entry the thickest and blackest of all, with details of his marriage and his three children – my grandfather and his two maiden sisters, who spent the first half of their lives ministering to their father's every wish and whim, and on his death, suitably rewarded, took up their residence in a Mediterranean country, where they lived happily if respectably to a ripe old age, upholding the Protestant religion and fighting cruelty to animals.

The next page was assigned to my grandfather, CHARLES ALBERT TRETHOWAN, 1870-1946, in much smaller letters. My grandfather, I believe, was an inoffensive, loving man, who tended the family fortune as best he could and devoted himself to his wife, his duties as magistrate, and his garden. He married Charlotte Victoria Matcham, 1877-1939, the daughter of a Yorkshire baronet. She was a gay, witty creature — as a hostess much loved by Edwardian society and on several occasions by King Edward himself. Her husband doted on her, obeyed her every whim, and turned a gallant blind eye when necessary. She loved children, but mainly, it was said, when they were little: she tended, I believe, to lose interest when they were six or seven. A psychiatrist might make something of this to explain the family. I'll leave you to do your own diagnoses. The offspring of this marriage were: ELIZABETH ALEXANDRA, 1898-1955; LAWRENCE EDGAR, 1900-   ; SYBILLA JANE, 1905-   ; CATHERINE SIEGLINDE, 1908-   ; and LEO VICTOR, 1911-   . The date of my father's death had not yet been inserted, but no doubt Sybilla, with the zeal of the survivor, was already scrabbling around for the printer's ink.

From now on one got a page to oneself only if one produced offspring. Aunt Eliza, for all her honours and talents, missed out. On Lawrence's page, however, it was recorded that he married first in 1918 Florence Emily Horsthorne, 1901-34, and produced a son, Wallace Abercrombie Trethowan, born 1919, missing, presumed dead 1944. And, second, in 1946, Lily Beatrice Cowper, born 1920, divorced 1954, by whom he had issue Peter Clement Trethowan, born 1947. My cousin Pete. Lawrence's page also recorded worldly honours — his election to the Royal Society of Literature, his knighthood (both ludicrous but very British elevations).

My Aunt Syb's page was shorter. It recorded her marriage in 1936, her divorce in 1942, and the sole offspring, Mordred Winston Foley, born 1941. My cousin Morrie.

The page also recorded the most notable of her theatrical works.

My father's page recorded his marriage in 1945 to Virginia Godrich, and her death in 1958. You will observe that he was already in his mid-thirties by the time of his marriage, and you may like to connect this marriage with Lawrence's loss of an heir in 1944. My father, naturally, denied any connection, and claimed that my sister and myself were not afterthoughts but long-delayed intentions. In any case, as you will have seen, Lawrence stole a march on him by marrying the following year and producing a replacement heir before he did. Anyway, my birth was recorded, Peregrine Leo, 1948-   and that of my sister, Cristobel, 1951-   , but I did not get a page to myself on which my marriage was recorded, or the birth of our son. I did not expect it: I had not, as you may say, paid my subscription. My father's page also recorded two or three of his less unsuccessful musical works, and the fact that he had served on the Arts Council Music Panel, 1958-60. Wowee!

My Aunt Kate got no page to herself: she had never married, nor even done anything with her life except make a fool of herself before one hundred thousand people at Nuremberg in 1938. The last page belonged to my cousin Peter, Lawrence's heir, recording his marriage to Maria-Luisa Gomez da Silva, and the birth of children Pietro 1971, Elena 1973, Mario 1975, Alessandro 1976, and Emilia 1978. My God! I thought. And all done in singles!

I closed the bible and went on my way, down the gloomy wide corridors hung with portraits and occasional etchings of industrial England in my great-grandfather's time (Hepplethwaite's Mill, Preston, 1854, and the like). Finally I reached the door that opened into the Gothic wing of Harpenden – my father's wing, my once and nevermore home.

I had figured out already which room my father was likely to have used for his 'experiments' – the high-ceilinged sitting-room on the ground floor. Ideal for the purpose, and much too large for him and Cristobel alone – no doubt they had moved their living quarters up to the first floor. I needn't have bothered figuring this out, for the entrance to the whole wing was guarded – by, happy memory, PC Smith, of my childish apple-stealing days; still PC Smith, but heavier and slower.

'You can't come in here, sir, not unless you're sent for. Special,' he intoned, looking immensely complacent. I showed him my card. 'Oh, sorry sir, Mr Perry, isn't it? Well, well . . . sir. I wouldn't ever have believed . . . The Superintendent is expecting you. In the old sitting-room. Straight through there, sir. But you'll remember the way, I s'pose.'

Yes. I remembered the way. I thanked him, and marched in.

My father, of course, had long since been taken down and hauled off to the morgue, so you will be spared horrific descriptions of purple faces and . . . well, do it yourself, if you fancy that kind of thing. All I saw was a splendid array of ropes, belts, pulleys and hooks – rather like something out of a museum of early industrial objects. There were other things in the room, whose nature I could only guess at, but it was the strappado which caught my eye and dominated the room. Standing by the apparatus, pensively, looking in urgent need of recourse to *Varieties of Sexual Experience*, or some such tome, was my colleague Superintendent Hamnet, Tim.

'Hello, Tim,' I said.

'Perry!' The relief and welcome which lit up his face were immediately replaced by professional sympathy: 'I say, old boy, I really am sorry.'

'So am I,' I said. 'I don't expect I'll ever recover from it.'

He lost the expression at once, and looked suspicious. 'But I thought you weren't close?'

'We weren't. I'm not talking about the death of my father. I'm talking about my professional reputation.' I began expatiating aggrievedly on a theme which had been nagging at me all the way up on the train. 'Do you realize, Tim, that whatever I may do in the future: if I save the President of the US from a bomb attack, catch a whole posse of Mafia hit men, wipe out the international drug traffic, banish hard porn and soft porn and four-letter words from our streets – still when I retire everyone in the force is going to say: "That was old Perry Trethowan: it was his Dad who got done in while he was practising medieval tortures in chorus-girl's tights". And they'll guffaw, or snigger, or hide their grins behind their hands, depending on the type of chap they are. That's me, fixed, for all eternity.'

Tim Hamnet was an honest man, so he didn't attempt to argue with me.

'Well, as I say, I'm deeply sorry,' he said. 'Bit of a facer, I can see that. Best thing for all of us is if we can get it all over and done with as soon as possible, eh? The Chief mapped out your role, I suppose?'

'Hmm,' I said. 'Our conversation was brief.'

'Naturally all the heavy stuff I'll be doing myself,' said Tim. 'All the interviews, the on-the-spot stuff, getting the lab reports. And of course I'll keep you informed about that. All we wanted you to do really was – well, ingratiate yourself with this lot – sorry, with your family, get their confidence, nose out all the background stuff, the little family tensions and so on—'

'*All* you want me to do!' I expostulated. 'I tell you, in comparison infiltrating all the rival Middle East freedom fighters would be a piece of cake. But I'll do what I can. I've made the first hurdle: I'm invited to stay for the funeral.'

'I took that for granted,' said Tim.

'You shouldn't have. Take nothing for granted with this family. It *never* does the conventional, as a matter of principle. Well, you'd better give me the basic low-down.'

As I said it, I sighed, and Tim himself gave a grimace of distaste. He turned back to the apparatus that dominated the room.

'Well, this, as you'll have gathered, is a sort of do-it-yourself strappado. Know anything about strappado?'

'I've educated myself since Joe called,' I said. 'It's a Spanish Inquisition torture, still used by a few enlightened governments as late as the last century. Not that we can afford to feel superior these days, I suppose. Anyway, what you did was you strapped the bloke up by the wrists, usually tied behind his back, you drew him up to the ceiling, then either you left him, or – the real refinement – let him down with a great big wallop till he nearly hit the floor, practically wrenching his arms out of their sockets in the process. If he was unwilling to recant his heresies, or shop his liberal friends, you repeated the process, *ad nauseam* or, as in this case, *ad mortem*.' I paused. 'Poor old bugger. Still, you can't say he didn't bring it on himself.'

Tim tried hard to be tactful about the whole business. 'Did you . . . did you know he went in for this kind of thing?'

'I don't think it had gone anything like as far as this while I was around. It was mostly books then, I think. I remember once having lunch with him in Soho, and after lunch as we were walking along he plunged into a dingy little bookshop and came out with a parcel in plain brown paper. We were on the way to a matinée of *Peter Pan* at the time.'

'He doesn't sound such a bad old buffer.'

'He just wanted to see Captain Hook. Anyway, when he went for the raspberry fizz at the interval I opened the package. It was a book called *Secrets of the Torture Chamber*. Vividly illustrated. I had dreams about those illustrations for months afterwards. I've been against third-degree methods every since. I later found he had a whole shelf of them: histories of the Inquisition, books on the birch, the cat. Most of them were presented as serious social histories, with frequent implied tut-tuts. The hypocrisy was almost as nasty as the practices described. I suppose it had to be presented in that way then. Nowadays you can probably get much the same info in any number of the *Beano*.'

'So he'd only taken up with this sort of experiment in the last few years?'

'So my Aunt Sybilla tells me.'

'Hardly a very wise recreation for a man of seventy.'

'You said it. Still, pensioners get some funny ideas, and

my papa was a bundle of nothing but. Come on, show me how the thing works.'

'Well,' said Tim Hamnet, going over to a pair of heavy leather wristguards on the end of two strong ropes. 'The first thing is to strap your arms into this, right? Not altogether easy if you're on your own, but these were no doubt designed specially and it's perfectly possible – I did it myself a minute or two ago. Your dad at least had the sense not to tie his hands behind his back first. Now, once you've done that, you can start the motor with your foot.'

He flicked the switch of the motor on the floor, then walked two paces away and grabbed hold of the heavy wristlets. The apparatus of ropes and belts moved slowly but inexorably, and gradually Tim was lifted, inch by inch, to the high ceiling, the weights on the other ends of the ropes being aided by the power-driven belts from the motor. When Tim was hanging full-length at the highest point there was a pause of about a minute. Then, as the machine momentarily cut out, Tim's weight immediately exceeded that of the balancing weights and he plunged to earth – but, letting go of the wristlets halfway, he landed nimbly on the floor.

'Christ, be careful, Tim. I never knew you were a gymnast.'

'No harm done. I tried that out before you came. But I wouldn't want to do it too often. Now – see the position of the wristlets now? Seven feet or so from the floor. Your father was a smaller man than you, Perry. His feet didn't quite touch the floor, however nasty the wrench he'd given himself. Hear that machine? It's starting off again. We're going through the whole process again. Now – note that when he's dangling, he can't switch the machine off with his foot. The only way to do that is when you're up at the ceiling – with that—'

He pointed to a white cord, which should have stretched from the on-off switch on the motor to a pulley in the ceiling.

'He could pull that when he was at the top, and he'd just be given one last bump.'

'Bloody daft idea!' I said. 'Practically inviting himself to have one more than he ought.'

'Not entirely daft, though,' said Tim. 'Since it was operated by the hand it was probably more reliable than something operated by the foot. Except that—'

And he pointed to what I already could hardly fail to have noticed: the cord from the ceiling had been neatly cut, and was dangling free. The other end trailed like a dead snake across the floor. I went over.

'Boffins finished?' I asked.

Tim nodded. I took the cut ends and brought them together. It had been sliced at a height of two feet or so from the floor. I looked at the ends: the cord was depressed into the centre, as if cut with scissors rather than a knife. I looked up again at the apparatus of belts and weights, and at the sturdy little motor.

'It's homemade,' said Hamnet.

'Really?' I said. 'I thought he might have picked it up at Harrods' toy department.'

'Tell me, Perry, what sort of chap was your father?'

'I suppose you mean apart from the sado-masochistic cum transvestite kinks he had?' I rested my foot on the little motor, and thought for a bit. 'Well, first of all, he was a very, very minor composer — so minor as to be virtually an amateur. I'll tell you what I think: he was the youngest, and I think he looked at the elder ones in the family, found we'd already got two artists and a writer and decided a composer was all there was left to be.'

This idea had first come to me as a boy, in the school holidays. HMV had just issued, with British Council support, an LP of my father's song-cycle *Dolores*, to words by Swinburne. Despite the best efforts of Alexander Young and a group of chamber musicians, it had received lukewarm reviews. But my father was delighted with it, absolutely chuffed. Listening to it, perforce, over and over again, I decided first, that my father had no feeling for words, then that he had no aptitude for music either.

Anyway, I gave Tim a run-through of my father's career,

which necessarily touched at several points on the careers and fame of the family as a whole. I mentioned their first scandalous success in 1929: it was called *The Somme*, and it was a sort of mixture of words, music, décor and scenic effects to which they all contributed. The intention was to lampoon the leaders of the First World War and crucify them for their conduct of it — by then hardly a new theme. But the way they did it was certainly novel: my Aunt Eliza painted some scarifying murals for the Wigmore Hall, which remained spotlit throughout; Sybilla organized some terrifying battle effects; my father (still in his teens, and at the Guildhall School) provided satirical settings of patriotic poems by Brooke and Julian Grenfell; Lawrence read his own poems from the ceiling (as if he were one of the better, dead, First World War poets). The newspapers loved it, and them: they were copy, to be applauded or pelted with journalistic mud. They went on loving them through the 'thirties, when they threw a succession of bohemian house-parties (my grandfather presiding benevolently, if bewilderedly) and put on two more examples of what I suppose today would be called 'total theatre'. Though their reputations waned, as far as the newspapers were concerned their star never entirely faded. Lawrence produced nothing of interest after the Second World War, Aunt Sybilla went into acidulated retirement, Aunt Eliza (admittedly still at the height of her powers) died in 1955.

Meanwhile my father never recovered from being an infant prodigy. His Stravinskyish settings of Brooke were followed by works derivative of other composers. I think he is seen at his best in his incidental music for a revival of Wilde's *Salome*, starring some 'thirties vamp whose name I have forgotten. True, he challenged Richard Strauss on his own ground, and was resoundingly beaten, but still, there was something in the subject that brought out the best of his meagre talents. And that something was something really very nasty. But this merely relative failure was no more than a flash in the pan. Of recent years he had produced nothing much at all: the last I heard of was a *Hymn of Tribute* on the occasion of the Silver Jubilee – it was commissioned by nobody and as far as I know played by nobody either, so the Monarch was spared.

All this I told Tim Hamnet.

'That's very interesting—' he said.

'Liar. It's the pathetic record of a ninth-rate talent.'

'—but what I really wanted was some idea of his . . . his personality. What sort of chap he was.'

'He was a snivelling little scrap of humanity, without a generous bone in his body. He was jealous of other people's success, always wanting to make a splash in the world but lacking the talent, guts and perseverance needed to achieve anything. He was a bad husband, a bad father and a frightful composer. Anything else?'

'I won't come to you next time I need a reference,' said Tim, who looked genuinely shocked. 'If I were you, Perry, I wouldn't go around saying that kind of thing.'

'Why not? I was at a lecture on "The Use and Abuse of the Laws on Sus" last night – at Scotland Yard, surrounded by policemen. I don't have a twin and it wasn't my double – doubles don't come easy at six feet five and seventeen stone. I talked to at least twelve people I know well and went for a pint with them afterwards. If you know of a better alibi, I don't.'

'I didn't mean that,' said Tim. 'I meant with the family. I should play down your opinion of him, if you want to get in with them again.'

'*You* want me to get in with them again. Apart from Cristobel, I shall rest happy if I see nary a one of them again for the rest of my life. As far as what I say or don't say is concerned, I'll play it by ear. It's perfectly possible that by the time he died my father was loathed to desperation by everyone in this house – in which case I won't get far by applying the soft soap. As I see it, the whole case probably hangs on the state of family relationships at the time of his death.'

'Agreed. By the way, you've never told me how you broke with him. Was he brutal?'

'I'd like to have seen him try. I was bigger than him by the time I was thirteen. And to be perfectly fair, as I always am, there was never much of that, even when I was small. His nastiness within the family was always of a much more subtle sort than that. No, the break came partly because I chose a career which did not measure up to the family's standards of eccentricity. This caused a running battle that went on for several months. Then one day, in the course of this, I came upon my father listening to a rather peculiar record. Remember the Savernake mob?'

'East Enders. Particularly nasty lot. Violent.'

'That's them. Most of 'em got life about fifteen years ago. There was a lot of gang warfare, and they specialized in getting hold of their opponents and using especially nasty forms of violence on them. Of course nowadays they've all got Open University degrees in Sociology and write incomprehensible letters to *The Times*. Well, my papa had got hold of tape-recordings of their torture sessions, things that were produced at the trial. And when I came on him, listening to them, and gloating, I—'

But we were interrupted by the chiming of the clock from the Elizabethan wing, a sound well remembered from childhood.

'Well, I suppose you can guess the sort of thing I said. I've got to go. If habits haven't changed in this house, it's now that The Family gathers for sherry. Sherry and Dinner are always taken together, otherwise they go their own ways. This is my best chance to catch them in the same place, so I shall consider myself on duty, as it were. By the way, do you know how my sister is?'

'Well, she was pretty hysterical, as you can imagine, after she found him. We got a few things out of her – about the time she found him, and so on. But she kept breaking down, so the family doc sedated her and she was put to bed. I think she's woken up since, but she's still a bit groggy, I gather.'

'OK. Sister can wait. I'll go and pour dry sherry and tepid epitaphs over my father's corpse.' I looked around the room.

'Really, after all this, I can't think of much pleasant to say about him.'

'You haven't seen the half,' said Tim. 'Just come and look at this.'

He led me over to a far corner, to an apparatus obviously still under construction. It didn't need much esoteric knowledge to conclude that this was a rack, and probably the work of the same ingenious gentleman who had designed the strappado. But I wasn't going to let Tim expound the workings of the rack to me: I'd had about as much embarrassment from the extended family as a man wants in one day. I made for the door, but I turned there and said:

'Watch it, Tim. One can develop a relish for that kind of thing. What's a well-brought-up policeman like you doing, getting involved with a family like mine?'

CHAPTER 4

TRETHOWANS AT MEAT

'I've been looking, ' said Aunt Sybilla, while Aunt Kate poured me a large sherry, 'for the printer's ink. To record your father's sad death, you know, Perry dear. And it occurs to me that we have entries to make up about you too, isn't that right?'

So: I was helping them; I had paid my subscription. I sipped my sherry (which was wine-seller's bulk, the sort of thing I drank at home, but decidedly not what used to be drunk in this house) and did my best to respond in friendly kind.

'That's right, Aunt Sybilla. I am married, and we have a son. But at the moment we are—'

'Oh dear – not separated?'

'Only physically. My wife is doing a degree at Newcastle, and our little boy is with her because my working hours are so unpredictable.'

'Really?' Aunt Sybilla's voice resumed some of its usual vinegarish tone. 'A policeman with a wife doing a degree! Quite original. What is it in – something *worthy*, and socially *rele*vant, I suppose? Like eco*nom*ics, or soci*ol*ogy?'

'Arabic,' I said.

Even Aunt Sybilla could make nothing of Arabic, and she retired for the moment defeated.

Not all the family had arrived yet. Lawrence was there, and showing some signs that he might be getting over his 'off day'; at any rate, though saying little, he was managing to clutch a sherry glass and convey it stiffly to his lips now and then with obvious enjoyment. Kate was standing to attention by the mantelpiece, a stance I remembered well, and the only other occupant of the room was Sybilla's son, my cousin Morrie (which is a ghastly name, but not half so ghastly as Mordred, the name that was inflicted on him at birth).

Mordred was a smallish man, dressed with a degree of pernicketiness, with a smiling, ingratiating, permanently youthful manner. He was, indeed, very much as I remembered him, on holidays from school — always looking as if he cleaned his teeth three times a day, and worried about ingrowing toenails. Morrie had had, I gathered, various short-term engagements in foreign universities, teaching English, but was now at leisure. What he was doing with his leisure, apparently, was vaguely researching for a book on — alas — the Trethowan family. And the awful fact is, it would probably have quite a good sale. I confess I could never actually *like* Morrie, but I came close to it when we shook hands and he said: 'Awfully embarrassing for you, old chap,' because he was the only member of the family who did seem to understand that.

It was Morrie who resumed the conversation now.

'It's terribly good to see you again, Perry, back with us all. I suppose it wouldn't do to ask you how things are going — over there—' and he jerked his head in the direction of the Gothic wing.

'I can't tell you much, I'm afraid. You realize I'm in rather a difficult position — neither fish nor fowl.'

'At least,' said Sybilla, 'they will have realized by now that it was an accident.'

'Well, no—' I began. But Lawrence had suddenly burst into spasmodic life.

'Accident? What was an accident?' He was so agitated he spilled sherry down his shirt front.

'I'm talking about Leo's going,' said Sybilla, her acidulated distinctness intended to contrast with his own slurred articulation. 'I'm saying that Leo's going was an accident.'

'Yes. Of course it was an accident. Pure accident.' Uncle

39

Lawrence subsided slowly, then suddenly said: 'Has Leo gone, then?'

'Yes, dear. You'll understand in the morning,' said Aunt Kate.

I stuck to my guns after this interruption, and resumed: 'I'm afraid you'll have to put the idea of an accident out of your minds. Almost definitely it was murder.'

'Oh, goody,' said Aunt Kate.

Aunt Sybilla, however, showed her displeasure. She retreated into the gauzy drapes which were her habitual costume, and sipped her sherry in a pouty way, as if it wasn't mother's milk to her. 'There's something awfully un-Trethowan about having a *policeman* in the house, and one of the family, too, talking about *murder* with such *horr*ible calm.' She sighed. 'It's like one of those television serials, about Liverpool or somewhere. Well, I won't ask any more tactless questions, but I shall rely on you, Peregrine, to see that the whole thing is *over* as soon as possible. We are none of us young. Lawrence, in particular, is not younger than the rest of us. We simply can't stand the fuss and vul*gar*ity of investigations of this sort. Meanwhile, after dinner I shall ring up my friends in Fleet Street.'

At this point we were interrupted. A door opened somewhere in the distance and there hit the ears a screaming, thumping din, which gradually came nearer and nearer.

'Oh dear, the Squealies,' said Aunt Sybilla. 'Peter's brood, you know, Perry. They're only allowed out of their part of the house once a day, at sherry time, so they won't worry you, or hinder your friend's investigations.'

'They're always getting out,' said Aunt Kate. 'They need a bit of discipline.'

I was inclined to agree when the hideous din, like an armoured regiment crossing a railway line, finally landed up with a bump at the sitting-room door, which opened to admit a screeching, fighting, filthy mass of half-clothed juvenile humanity. Each one was passionately conducting three quarrels at once at the top of his voice, the elder ones pushing the faces of the smaller, the smaller kicking the ankles of the elder. As they got into the room their language suddenly changed from street Italian to English. One of them shrilled 'There's Gran'pa,' and they swarmed over him like the locusts over Egypt, crying 'Give me a sweetie, Gran'pa,' 'Me too, Gran'pa,' and the like. And the odd thing was, Uncle Lawrence seemed to like it: he woke up, patted them on the head, said a few 'Who? Who?'s (understandably, I thought) and began scuffling around in his pockets for sweets. This was clearly a nightly ritual: Aunt Kate had taken Lawrence's sherry glass and held tight to his chair as soon as the sound of the infant army had been heard in the distance. I confess I did not regard them with anything like Lawrence's benevolence, except in one vital respect: this ghastly brood, three of them male, made it quite certain I would never inherit the family abode. And that was quite a lot to be grateful for.

Bringing up the rear of this invasion were the parents. My cousin Peter strolled lazily along, oblivious of the row. He was wearing a denim suit (Oh God! a denim suit!) which he bulged out of fore and aft, over and under. Though hardly a year older than me he had a general surface flab that was nasty – as if he were an Italian *paterfamilias* of forty or so, of whom years of pasta and sweet cakes had taken their toll (which no doubt *was* part of the problem with Pete, too). His flab was probably white and jellyfishy, though. His face was set in a self-satisfied sneer: he came over, nodded, said: 'Heard you were back, Perry,' with a notable lack of enthusiasm, then went and poured himself a drink.

He was followed by his wife. You won't need to be told that she was pregnant again.

All I'd heard about Maria-Luisa was of her origins: her father had been a Spanish or Portuguese gypsy, her mother a Sicilian peasant, bastard daughter of a German tourist. All Europe had contributed to the making of Maria-Luisa, and you'd have thought all Europe could have made a better job of it. She was fat, slovenly, foul-tempered, with a large vocabulary of Latin abuse but not, apparently, a single word of English. She understood it, though, giving Sybilla yet further chances of employing her condescending, over-distinctly articulated tone of voice.

'Grappa Julia, Maria-Luisa? Oh dear, we're out. I must tell McWatters to reorder. Will you have a Cinzano?'

Maria-Luisa muttered bitterly, then said: '*Si.*'

We were not introduced. But over her drink she stared at me with frank peasant curiosity.

So here I was, in the bosom of my family. That is all the family you will be introduced to for the moment, except for my sister Cristobel, and I can tell you, standing there with the whole lot around me — not to mention the family portraits alternately lowering and simpering from the walls — made me as uneasy as a mouse at a cat's tea-party. This was what I had been running away from for fourteen years, and now suddenly I found I had run full circle and here I was again in the middle of them, being watched, appraised, and no doubt found wanting. It wasn't that I felt they were a whole lot more intelligent than I am: it would be false modesty to pretend I did. But I did think they were a whole lot more cunning, and what's more they were a whole lot better in the picture as far as the murder was concerned. What if they were all in it — had ganged up together for some odd Trethowanish reason? I think my cousin Pete sensed my uneasiness, because he said nastily: 'Well, it takes a death to bring the family together, doesn't it?'

Two of them, at least, felt the need to cover this over a bit, and Mordred said, 'Anyway, it's good to have you back, Perry,' and Aunt Kate said, 'It's just as if you never went away.' (Oh, no, it's not, Aunt Kate. Not for me.)

'Life is strange,' mused Sybilla, who was a dab hand with a platitude. 'Who would have thought, last evening, that within twenty-four hours we would have lost one, and gained one!'

Maria-Luisa, for some reason, let out a raucous, spiteful laugh.

'What had my father been like, these last few days?' I asked. 'Perfectly normal?'

'Perfectly well,' said Sybilla, understandably rejecting my adjective. 'In the pink of health. Otherwise he would hardly have—'

'No. Quite,' I said. 'What had his life been like, in the years since I was here? You must remember that I know very little of his routines.'

'Oh, not much changed. He pottered a little in the garden – we only have two men there now. He liked a trip to London now and then: his club, the bookshops – you know. He did a little composing – he was never one of those *fertile* geniuses, though, was he? Then we all have to chip in a bit in the house these days. Really a *terrible* bore, but what can we do? The McWatterses are all we have living in, and they *insist* on two days off a week.'

'Awfully inconsiderate of them,' I said.

'We take it in turns to cook,' put in Kate.

'That's right,' resumed Sybilla. 'Maria-Luisa gives us some of her *i*nteresting Italian and Iberian dishes. The oily tang of the South – so refreshing! Then Mordred was in Sweden for a time, you know, and he does some enchanting things with herrings. And then Kate, too—'

'I cooked last night,' burbled Kate, full of herself. 'I go in for interesting combinations. Most cooks are so unadventurous. I gave them meat-loaf with caramel sauce. Everyone said it was scrumptious!'

For the first time I felt a twinge of pity for my father. To go to Hell with a belly full of meat-loaf and caramel sauce was a fate worse than even I would wish on him.

'It was *quite* delicious, Kate dear,' said Sybilla, winking at me. 'So your father had his day as well—'

'It was always tinned ham and salad,' said Kate, pressing her superiority. 'That was almost cheating. And Chrissy had to wash the salad things.'

'Well, he did his best. As we all do. Except poor Lawrence, who since his stroke really *can't* manage his arms and legs well enough, even on his good days.'

'My poor old Pop, he ain't what he used to be,' said Pete, with a wholly synthetic sympathy. 'My poor old Pop has been through it.'

'Been through it?' suddenly boomed Lawrence from his wheelchair, where he had apparently been dozing happily. 'By God, yes. By God we went through it. Nobody who wasn't in the trenches can have an idea of what it was like. That's what I tried to convey: "The mud, the mud, the blend of earth and gore!"; "The shrill, demented choirs of wailing shells". That's what it was like! A living hell! You young people know nothing! Nothing!'

It was my uncle's habit, as the observant of you may have noted, to mingle a line or two of his own turgid sonnets with lines by more talented poets of the First World War. It was only years after I left home, when I started dipping into histories and memoirs of the time, that I discovered the true authors of lines I'd known from boyhood, and had been convinced were the work of Lawrence Trethowan.

Lawrence's reawakening did not go unnoticed by the Squealies, who had been fighting happily among themselves in the far corner, but now regathered to clamber all over him and pick his pockets of 'sweeties'. Luckily, in the midst of this nauseating performance McWatters came in to announce dinner, and their mother collected them up in her brawny arms and removed them to their own wing, squeaking and bawling until the door was finally shut on them and it felt like Armistice Day, 1918.

As we all trooped in to dinner, Sybilla took my arm in her bony claw and whispered: 'You needn't worry. None of us is "on" tonight. Mrs McWatters is a jewel.'

And certainly the food, though traditional, was first rate. But we were an ill-assorted gathering to eat it. Maria-Luisa talked only to her husband, keeping up a constant stream of comment, complaint and imprecation in what sounded like gutter Italian, probably with bits of something else thrown in (at any rate, it certainly didn't sound to my

44

ears like the Tuscan language spoken by a Roman tongue). Pete just said '*si*' and '*no*' and '*basta*', and looked bored and contemptuous, though he forked his food in with enthusiasm. I had relieved Aunt Kate of the job of wheeling Lawrence in, and when I had placed him at the head of the table he had looked round and said: 'Capable young chap. Who is he?' Then he had relapsed into concentrated eating. McWatters had left two tureens of soup on the table, and we served ourselves.

'Not what you were used to in other days, Perry dear,' said Sybilla, leaning over almost intimately. 'We thought it was difficult with servants then, but now it's simply impossible!'

'It wouldn't be like this if we had won the war!' suddenly barked Aunt Kate.

There was an immediate silence round the table, even from Maria-Luisa, who evidently understood more than might have been expected. They all looked at me, to see how I would take it. Me, I was used to my Aunt Kate, and her unorthodox arrangement of loyalties. I went on eating my soup. The atmosphere relaxed.

'*Dear* Kate!' sighed Sybilla. 'There's a touch of her old self back tonight!'

I smiled briefly. 'You're all very much as I remember you, you know. And it sounds as if my father hadn't changed greatly. You don't think he had any special worries when he died, do you?'

'Dear me, no,' said Sybilla, vaguely, the drape around her wrist trailing in the soup. Then she perked up. 'But he might easily have had some that we didn't know about. Do you think he took his own life?'

'No,' I said firmly. Then I went on in my plodding policemanlike fashion: 'Had there been any tensions, dissensions, disagreements over the last few days?'

'He's inquisiting us!' chortled Kate. 'Just like in a book.'

'Not that I know of,' said Mordred, who was turning out to be easily the most sensible of the lot. 'But then I'm a

45

bit out of it. If it wasn't brought to table here, I wouldn't have noticed.'

I turned to Aunt Sybilla. 'You probably saw more of him. Was there anything that you noticed?'

'Well, no, Perry dear. Otherwise I'd have said. Of course, you know us. We're very much creatures of instinct.' (Oh yes – pure children of nature: with resident butler and cook, a dozen cleaners, two gardeners, and several acres of house to be natural in.) 'If we *feel* anything, we say it out. So much better to be *open*. So if there had been any *major* row, I'd certainly have heard of it . . . Certainly.'

The fact is, the way this bear-garden is arranged, with each group going its own way in its own wing, and each wing miles from the other wings, it was perfectly possible for major rows, wide-ranging conspiracies or out-and-out cold war to take place and yet be kept secret, provided a moderately good face was put on on 'public' occasions. Which meant, I took it, at sherry time and over dinner. I chewed over this as I enjoyed Mrs McWatters's excellent steak and kidney pudding.

I chewed over something else as well, and that was the feeling I was beginning to get that the family, and Sybilla in particular, was welcoming me back into the happy group, reinstating me in the family Bible and all, because they thought that I could protect them in some way from the consequences of having a murder in the family. Nobody loves a policeman these days except when a crime might occur or has occurred, and the Trethowans were less 'law and order' people than most. But now I was a friend in high places, to make sure their cosy little world was not shattered. As you can understand, I imagine, this sort of protection was one thing I had no intention of giving them. So as we gracefully spooned our syllabub into our (not noticeably impaired by the tragedy) digestive systems, I made a frightfully official-sounding clearing-of-the-throat noise, and started actually to address them all:

'If you don't mind, Aunt Syb . . . and, er, Uncle Lawrence . . . there's just one thing I'd like to say, now we're all together. I'm very grateful to you for welcoming me back home as you have. And of course for your sympathy. And I shall certainly do all I can to advise you in the present difficult situation. And if possible to help you. But what I can't do—'

But I was interrupted. From the distance there came once more the hair-raising sound of infant strife, a yowling, rolling, thumping sound that seemed to be approaching us irresistibly like the armies of Genghis Khan, spreading havoc and destruction in their wake. Peter and Maria-Luisa compounded matters by screaming at each other in their own queer linguistic modes of communication, and it ended by Peter going disgruntledly out just as the Squealies were at the door. Aunt Sybilla raised her eyebrows.

'You were saying, Perry dear?'

But at that moment there was yet another interruption. The door to the hall opened, and in came PC Smith. Looking more than a little overwhelmed (for this was not just gentry, remember, but his own particular gentry), he crossed the great open space of the dining-room and, standing by Aunt Sybilla's chair, said in a low voice:

'Superintendent Hamnet would be glad to see you as soon as possible after dinner, Miss Trethowan.'

It was as if he'd made an indecent suggestion.

'Perry!' squawked Aunt Sybilla, her eyes bulging with outrage. 'I do think I might have been spared this!'

I banged my fist on the table with a force that raised the glassware and crockery an inch.

'What I was just about to say was that the one thing I cannot and will not do is protect you from the normal processes of the law in a case of murder. Nothing can protect anyone from that – except diplomatic immunity.'

'Then I must set about getting it with all despatch,' said Sybilla, throwing down her napkin and stalking from the room.

The meal, not surprisingly, more or less broke up after this. Maria-Luisa poured herself another large glass of wine and stomped out after her maniacal brood. Aunt Kate wheeled a mumbling, dribbling Lawrence off to bed with a reproachful 'He's *not* to be upset, you know.' Only Mordred seemed inclined to linger. He poured us both a glass of port, and I was about to settle down to a little chat before going up to my sister when McWatters came in with a little servant's cough (so different from a policeman's magisterial clearing of the throat) and said: 'Oh, Mr Peregrine, sir, there's a phone call for you.'

'Probably the Yard,' I said, getting up. 'You're sure it's not really for Hamnet?'

'Oh yes, sir. It's for you. Actually sir, the leddy said she was your wife.'

'My God!' I said. I hurried out to the extension I'd seen in the hall, then changed my mind and asked McWatters if there wasn't anywhere more private.

'There's Sir Lawrence's study,' he said doubtfully. 'But mebbe it'd be best if you were to use the one in the old butler's pantry.' He led me down a corridor, through the great baize door, down a staircase, and into the well-remembered, high-ceilinged domestic palace which my great-grandfather Josiah had deemed suitable to minister to his needs. You could have cooked the Coronation dinner in here. But McWatters went to a side door and showed me into a considerable and well-equipped apartment, suitable to the dignity of an Edwardian butler.

'If you'll take up the receiver, sir, I'll put you through in a moment.'

Within thirty seconds I heard a click and said: 'Jan?'

'Perry! Home is the sailor, home from the—'

'Cut that out! How did you know I was here?'

'I read about the death in the papers. It sounded fishy. I knew it was your day off, so I kept ringing home. Then suddenly I put two and two together. The sentimental little lad has gone back for the funeral baked meats.'

'Nothing of the sort. I am here under orders and under protest.'

'That's exactly what I guessed, actually. Knowing Joe.

48

So my deduction from the newspaper report that all is not quite quite, so to speak, was right?'

'Nothing is ever quite quite with my family. You've no idea how dire it all is.'

'Never fear. Help is on the way. Daniel and I are coming for the weekend. You know how I've always wanted to meet your f—'

'*No*,' I said. 'No, you are *not*.'

'Don't tell me they'd refuse to meet me?'

'*I* refuse to let *you* meet *them*.'

'There's obviously room for us. I bet we could both fit into your bedroom.'

'There's room for the Eighth Army in my bedroom. That is not the point.'

'Perry, I know you can't be officially on the case, so why are you being so appallingly stuffy?'

'Because,' I said, 'I do not choose to bring my wife and son to a house where a murder has just been committed and in which a murderer is still at large.'

This stumped her a bit. There was a long silence.

'So long as it's not that you're ashamed of me in front of your family,' Jan said, rather feebly.

'You know perfectly well I'm ashamed of my family in front of you.'

'Well, that's all right, then. That's as it should be. Perhaps it is best if we actually stay in the village.'

'You'll have a job. "The Village" is about ten houses.'

'And a pub. The Marquis of Danby.'

'That fleabitten hostelry. I had my first pint there.'

'Probably it'll be some kind of anniversary, then.'

'Don't be deceived by the grand name: it's a tiny country inn with two cramped bars. They certainly won't take guests.'

'They certainly do. The AA book says so.'

'My God. It's probably been tarted up.'

'Better that than fleas, anyway. Well, so I'll collect Daniel after lectures are over, give him something to eat to keep him happy, and then drive over in the early evening. Wasn't it lucky I got a place at Newcastle?'

'Jan, I still—'

'See you tomorrow. Love to the aunties and uncles!'

And she rang off. I sometimes win arguments with my wife, but never those conducted over the telephone. I shrugged my shoulders in irritation, and decided to go and have a good talk to Cristobel.

CHAPTER 5

CRISTOBEL

Cristobel – that's a bloody silly name to start with. Or silly spelling. Because it's pronounced perfectly normally, as in Pankhurst. That sort of silly-buggery runs in our family. Would you believe that my cousin Pete was supposed to be called Pyotr? Only the clergyman making a deliberate mistake at the font and standing Uncle Lawrence out that it couldn't be rectified saved him from that fate. And look at Kate. I sometimes wonder whether she wasn't conceived in a private box at Covent Garden, during one of the more missable sections of *Die Walküre*.

You mustn't think I'm not fond of Cristobel. I am in my own way. And she's worth all the rest put together. So bear this in mind if I am occasionally a little negative about her. She could irritate me – and she certainly irritated me in the course of this case. For a start she is a Girl Guide. I suppose she got this from Aunt Kate. Did I tell you that when Kate attended the Nuremberg Rally of 1938 she did so in Girl Guide's uniform? There was a great flurry of Brown Owls about that, and they were just getting down to a delicious Discussion of Principle on the subject in the highest Guiding circles when Hitler invaded Poland and out she had to go. They all thought it very unsporting of Hitler. Well, Cristobel is by now a Brown Owl or a Grey Squirrel or something of the sort, and she is rather a lumpy, earnest, well-meaning sort of girl, one of those people who can probably light a fire with twigs but might well destroy acres of national parkland by doing so.

After that rather unsatisfactory conversation with my wife I went up through the green baize doors and into the main part of the house. McWatters was just entering the dining-room as I passed through the hall, and I wondered whether he'd been listening in on the hall extension. Then I went up the great staircase (which seemed to have been conceived for corpulent fin-de-siècle monarchs to make an entrance down, arm in arm with their consorts) and to my bedroom. Dear Aunt Sybilla had told McWatters to put me in my old room, but he had had the sense to realize I would not much want a room in the Gothic wing, even had the police allowed it, so I'd been given the principal guest bedroom in the main block – an enormous room, inevitably, big enough to erect a circus tent in, with its own bath and shower and, of all things, John Martin's *The Destruction of Sennacherib* taking up most of the inner wall. I have grown up with nineteenth-century painting, it's very much part of me, but still I decided that *The Destruction of Sennacherib* was not under present circumstances the kind of interior decoration best calculated to cheer the faltering spirit. Alas, there was no question of taking it down, or turning its face to the wall. I walked round the room for a bit, tut-tutting at the thought of Jan's and Daniel's arrival; I got out my notebooks (part of my personal equipment for a case) but wrote nothing in them; then I decided to go along and have my talk to Cristobel.

Cristobel, after her hysterics, had been put in another guest-room only three doors from mine – hardly more than the length of Liverpool Street Station away. I tapped on the door. There was a long pause, and I stood picturing her there, frightened out of her wits. I had just reached down to open the door and put her out of her misery when there was a small 'Come in.'

She was lying in bed, very white against the sheet, and in that big room oddly and unusually small. She managed a frightened smile.

'Oh, hello, Perry. Is it you? I'm glad you've come.'

'Hello, Chris. How are you, old girl?'

'Getting over it. I hope to be up and about tomorrow.'

(Up and about is the sort of phrase Chris uses. She probably barges round the Guides' camps bellowing 'Rise and Shine'.)

'Don't you think about getting up yet. There's nothing you can do: the police have taken over the whole wing. Just you try and make a proper statement to Hamnet — he's the CID man — then stay put where you are.'

'The CID? Then it's definitely murder?'

'Oh yes, I'd say so. But you knew that, didn't you?'

Chris shook her head. 'I didn't know. I just couldn't believe — I mean, who would do anything like that? I mean — *like that*?'

'Somebody, my lass. So we'll just have to face up to it. Would you like to tell me what happened?'

'I suppose I can try, if I've got to tell the — *them*, tomorrow. Well, I went up to bed at my usual time.'

'When's that?'

'About half past ten. I have to get up early to do most of the housework before Daddy gets down. Got down. Anyway, when I went to bed, Daddy went . . . downstairs. To . . . well, you know. When he did it, it was always after I'd gone to bed, in case I was disturbed by the . . . bumps. He was awfully considerate like that.'

Charming olde-worlde courtesy, I thought. But I just nodded.

'Well, about a quarter past twelve I . . . er . . . still hadn't got to sleep—'

'Why?'

'No reason, I just hadn't. And so I came down to the kitchen to get an aspirin or something. It's on the first floor of the wing, you remember, and you can . . . hear. And so I heard, and I thought: this isn't right. He *never* did it for that long. And I ran downstairs into the Gothic room and—'

'Were the lights on?'

'Yes, very bright. And I saw—'

She stopped, sobbing, and I sat on the bed and put my

53

arms around her, like I did when our mother died. Eventually she calmed down and wiped her eyes.

'Did you notice the cut cord?' I asked.

Chris nodded. 'I dashed over and switched the thing off, and it – he – came down with a last bump and he seemed about six inches away and it was – horrible. I screamed and ran out of the wing into the house, and screamed and screamed.'

'Who came out to you first?'

'Oh dear. McWatters, I think. Did you know he wears a nightshirt? Oh no, you don't know him. Then Mrs Mac. Then – Mordred, I think, and later Sybilla.'

'What did they do?'

'Someone – McWatters, I think – ran to the Gothic wing, then dashed back and called the police. He told them to bring a doctor, but he must have known . . . I knew.'

'I see. Then they put you to bed?'

'Yes. They tried slapping me, and water, but Mordred said it was barbaric and the doctor would be here in a minute. So they got me to bed, and I don't remember much more. Eventually I talked a bit to the police, but I kept—'

'I know. Well, it's over now. Perhaps Hamnet won't need to talk to you again about that. I'll report back to him. Chris, what had things been like in the family recently?'

'Oh, you know, much as usual. We each lived in our own wings, but still – it isn't an easy house to live in, Perry.'

'I know,' I said.

'But I don't complain. It's always the way, isn't it? The men go off and do the glamorous and exciting jobs and the women get left behind looking after the older generation. It's always been like that and I suppose it always will be.'

Hmmm, well, I thought. I'd been getting stuff like this in letters from my sister recently, showing, I suppose, that this kind of lowest-common-denominator feminism has at last filtered down into the kind of magazine my sister reads. As the bandwagon grinds slowly to a halt, my sister hears of the movement. Now, the fact of the matter is that my sister stayed home with my father because she had no aptitude for any kind of interesting job and wanted to inherit what was going. Highly sensible reasons, of which I heartily approve, but no basis for a good feminist whine. My great-aunts, daughters of the redoubtable Josiah, may not have had much choice, but Chris did, and made it. And if anyone by some laughable contingency had offered Chris a glamorous and exciting job, she would have cast a pall of the humdrum over it within hours of signing on. Still, this wasn't quite the time for saying things like that.

'You say it wasn't easy. What especially do you mean? Had there been any rows, any big problems?'

'Nothing out of the ordinary, really. Aunt Kate has been very odd since her breakdown, as I suppose you'll have noticed.'

'Yes. But hardly *odder*. Better on the whole, I thought.'

'Perhaps. But you never know where you are. What else? Oh, people were always complaining about the Squealies. Then there was a great fuss over some picture or other—'

'Oh?'

'Aunt Sybilla was going to redecorate one of the guest-rooms. You know she sometimes feels her artistic talents aren't stretched to the full these days.' (When my sister says things like that there is not a hint of irony. I have heard her refer to our father as a great composer. She is a true Trethowan.) 'She went looking for something that was put up in a lumber-room when they first hung Aunt Eliza's pictures of the family in the drawing-room. But you know how it is. That was twenty-five or thirty years ago. They couldn't find the picture.'

'I see. What was it?'

'I don't know. Rossetti, or Holman Hunt, or somebody.'

'Did she think it had been stolen?'

'Oh – you know: she went around saying it was very *odd*, and telling Mordred he ought to do an inventory of the whole house – as if poor Morrie hasn't got enough to do with the family history. It would take years. Anyway, I wouldn't be surprised if it didn't turn up, in some room or other.'

'Very likely it will. There must be some nobody's been in since the builders moved out. So Father wasn't really at the centre of any of these rows, was he?'

'No, not really. He sort of stirred things up, now and then. Helped them along. Of course, it's awful to say things about him now he's dead . . .'

'If you don't, we'll probably never find out who did it.'

'No. Well, he said he thought we should get somebody qualified to do the inventory – implying poor Morrie wasn't, and that was a red rag to Aunt Sybilla. In any case, it's almost all Uncle Lawrence's property, in fact.'

'And he didn't want an investigation?'

'Oh, I think he did say it would be a good idea. But then I suppose he had one of his days, or something. Anyway, one way or another the whole idea got forgotten.'

'Chris, you've been with Father these last fifteen years. He wasn't an easy man to get along with, I know. Which of the family would you say hated him most?'

Chris thought for a bit. 'Well, I suppose you, Perry.'

'Apart from me,' I said impatiently. 'Let me tell you I have an absolutely cast-iron alibi, otherwise I wouldn't be here.'

'I wouldn't say anybody actually hated him,' said Cristobel, resuming her pensive pose. 'It sounds so melodramatic. I mean, he and Maria-Luisa sometimes had words about the Squealies. They're lovely children, but they must have been particularly trying to someone *musical*, don't you think? And Mordred was a *little* bit put out when he wanted the professional art historian in to do the inventory. Nothing more than that. He and Syb jogged along much as they always did.'

'And how did you get on with him, Cristobel?'

'All right. We went our own ways. I did most of the cooking and cleaning in this wing, but I had a lot of free time. I have the Guides and that. And I'm great friends with the vicar's wife, and I sing in the choir. He didn't interfere.

Most of us in this house go our own ways, you know. On the whole it works very well.'

I got up with a vague feeling of dissatisfaction.

'There's precious little to go on so far. Precious little in the way of possible motive. It just seems senselessly cruel and pointless.'

'Senseless? Do you mean a . . . a lunatic might have done it? Someone from outside? Or Aunt Kate?'

'I wasn't pointing at Aunt Kate,' I said. 'If she did it, I'd bet it was for a very good reason. Well – you'd better get some sleep now, Chris. I'll pass all this on to Hamnet, to spare you as much as possible tomorrow. If I were you I'd stop there and get a bit more of your strength back.'

I kissed her and moved over to the door. It was just as I was opening it that Cristobel came out with her most interesting idea so far.

'Perry,' she said, 'has it occurred to you that one of the Squealies might have done it? In play, I mean?'

CHAPTER 6

NIGHT PIECE

I went back in and closed the door.

'Do you think that's possible, Chris? Could they have got through the house without being seen?'

'I think so. It's a big house, and we live in our separate wings. You can hear people coming miles off and get out of the way. Uncle Lawrence would be the one they'd be most likely to meet, and you can certainly hear his wheels. Anyway, he's often in Kate's wing these days – he certainly was last night. She's the one who looks after him.'

'Kate implied they often got out.' (I realized this sounded like caged animals, but so be it.)

'They do. Not all that often, but they do. Mostly they play together. They're not . . . terribly well behaved.'

'So I noticed. They struck me as complete monsters. But do you think one of them might actually—'

'Well, of course, they wouldn't *realize* what they were doing. It would just be in fun, they'd think. But they are *awfully* naughty sometimes. They just don't think.'

'Do you think anyone could have used them? Put the suggestion into their minds? One of their parents . . . ?'

'Oh Perry! Of course not! Nobody could be so *wicked* as to use a little child like that!'

Poor innocent Cristobel! I saw I had distressed her. 'I expect you're right,' I said. 'Now you get a good night's sleep, Chrissy, and I'll see you in the morning.'

I went back to my room. I didn't feel ready for bed yet, and certainly not for sleep. I showered in a luxurious flow of water (none of your miserable modern trickles for Harpenden House) and soaped vigorously, as if to wash off the slime of such a homecoming. That was marvellous, but it was while I was doing it that my mind, still over-active, started to grapple with the odd feeling of dissatisfaction – something niggling away at the back of my mind that refused to come forward, you know how it is. Of course the whole day had not been of the sort to make me pirouette for joy, as you will have gathered, but there was something else – something that had not been quite . . . it was something, yes – that was when the feeling had begun – something connected with my talk with Cristobel.

It was while I was towelling myself down that it came to me: she wasn't relieved enough that I had come.

Now don't get the wrong idea about this. I suppose you're thinking that this is a big *macho* thing on my part: he wants little sister to sob on his chest and say 'Now you've come, Perry, I feel safe,' and all that stuff that flatters the male ego and may have some truth in it or no truth at all. He thinks she should have made him feel tough and capable and in control.

No, it's not that at all. But I know Cristobel, and just think yourself of the situation: here is a girl, not very bright or very confident, who has just found her father murdered in a peculiarly horrible manner; she is surrounded by nuts whom she cannot find very congenial or put any great trust in; along comes a brother, a policeman, whom she is fond of and who is (on the surface) pretty sure of himself and who ought to be a pillar of strength and reliability to her. You would expect her to be pleased, to feel a load off her mind – in short, to be relieved.

Now, I think Chrissy was pleased to see me as a person. And yet . . . I pinned it down: I wasn't convinced she was pleased to see me as a policeman.

And that was odd, and thought-provoking, and disturbing.

For some reason my mind went back to a talk I'd had with Cristobel ten years or so before. It was while I was still in the army, when I was thinking of going over to the CID.

And it was four years after I had flung myself out of this house, shouting at my father that he was a dirty-minded, sadistic mediocrity. I was giving Chris lunch in London, and I could see that she was lonely and unhappy, and rather nauseated by my father's tastes and habits. I urged her to get a job, but she resisted, and I could see that she was counting on the money from Father — such as it would be — to give her some kind of independence when he died. Anyway, I was a bit upset by her position in the house, and I actually suggested I try for a reconciliation with Father, so that I could visit her more often.

'Oh, I don't think that's at all possible,' Cristobel had said. 'He was *deeply* wounded.'

'What, at my calling him a sadist?'

'No. At your calling him a mediocrity.'

Well, that figured. Or had seemed to at the time. Still, I recalled that conversation now, and wondered if Cristobel had ever wanted a reconciliation between me and the family. At times like this, you know, nasty thoughts even about the comparatively near and dear do occur to one.

I put on pyjamas and went over to the desk, where my notebook lay, white and inviting. I opened the window: the night air outside was warm, even heavy. It was early autumn — season of mists and mellow fruitfulness. Or of decay and death, if you are in that frame of mind. I sat at the great Victorian desk, big enough to store a couple of bodies in, drew my notebooks towards me and took up my pen.

'Why *that* way?' was the first thing I wrote.

I'd told Joe that that was *just* the way one of my family *would* kill somebody, and I held by that. Still, almost any other way would have been quicker, cleaner, safer. Whoever did it must surely have been *seen* by my father to do it. And there was no guarantee that my father would not be heard, crying for help. I jotted down: 'Lights on.' It was a spectacular but exceedingly dangerous way of getting rid of anybody, and it almost suggested that the method was part of the point — that the murder was some kind of appropriate revenge, some ghastly tit-for-tat affair.

Which in its turn suggested some victim of my father's peculiarly perverted mind.

I next wrote: 'Scissors? Knife? Where are they?'

Whatever it was had been used, it was in effect the murder implement, and would have to be found, even if it brought us no closer to any particular individual. And that, to a practical policeman, immediately suggested an army of PCs swarming through the house. If a proper search of the house were to be made, let alone of the grounds, it would take days. Which would *not* please Aunt Sybilla. But perhaps I could suggest they search for the missing picture at the same time?

I wrote. 'Picture. Get description. Painter.'

Then I wrote: 'Financial situation. Not just Father's. Lawrence's. All the rest too.'

That, surely, Tim Hamnet would do. I hoped Chrissy would be left fairly well off – a tidy sum would be only her just deserts. My father, though, when I knew him, was not careful with money, even though he had always hated to be swindled. He was the last person in the world to care whether anybody else would be well off or hard up after he died. Lawrence *should* be very comfortably off. With the house, in the male line, went a hell of a lot of money. But these days, none of the whacking fortunes were quite what they were. There had been inflation, the house itself must be a terrible millstone, there was Peter, who seemed to have no visible means of support. Day-to-day living in the house seemed much more frugal than in my time. Was Lawrence becoming miserly in his old age, as so frequently happened, or were there solid reasons for the frugality? At least the house – that is, Lawrence – had tremendous assets, of every kind.

I wrote down: 'Pictures. Worth how much?'

The Times kept me informed of saleroom prices. Little-known Victorian painters were often fetching quite fantastic sums these days. Not to mention the moderns – and under Aunt Eliza's supervision quite a lot of first-rate stuff had been bought for Harpenden in the 'twenties and 'thirties. Interesting.

On the other hand, it was not immediately apparent how the financial state of the head of the family could have any bearing on the death of my father.

I got up and walked around a bit. There was this to be said about Harpenden: it gave you room to move about. Hour by hour, in fact, I felt myself expanding. Space itself took on a new dimension, and I felt in a relation to things quite different from the one I was in in the little flat in Maida Vale, where the three of us lived. Thinking about us I thought about Daniel, and thinking about Daniel I (most unfairly) thought about the Squealies. There was the possibility that one of them (*not* all together, surely — I could not imagine all five of them moving through the house with murderous stealth) had crept over to the Gothic wing and snipped through the cord. This would argue, I thought, a certain mechanical aptitude, or that the Squealy in question had watched my father 'at it' before. Not impossible. The eldest Squealy was — what? — about ten. Still, I didn't find it altogether probable. There was also the possibility that the murderer (or the Trethowans in general, closing ranks under attack, as was their wont) would put it about that that was what had happened. Even persuade one of the Squealies to confess. Though that might prove a highly dangerous course.

But so would be the other possibility: persuading a Squealy to do it and instructing it how. Hideously dangerous. But perhaps not quite so dangerous if the persuader were one of its parents.

It was just at this point in my perambulations about the great guest bedroom that I thought I heard something. I crossed to the window and stuck out my head: undoubtedly I had heard something, and what it was was sounds of fury, of altercation. And it wasn't difficult to guess where they came from. I stuck my feet into slippers and quick as a flash I was out of the room, down the great staircase, and out of one of the back doors. I pulled the door to: McWatters had given me all the necessary keys, so I could get back in. I made off through the garden, finding to my pleasure that I knew every tree, every flower-bed. The air was warm and still, the garden a mass of looming, menacing shapes, the moon through the trees highlighting the nearly bare branches. The leaves on the ground were like a pillow under my slippered feet. I skulked towards the Elizabethan wing.

The two wings on the back of the house were the Florentine wing (occupied by Sybilla and Mordred) and the Elizabethan (occupied by Peter and his brood). It required no great deductive genius to guess that if anyone was bawling their lungs out at twelve o'clock at night, it was likely to come from the Elizabethan wing. I darted from tree to tree, hugging the shade, shunning the moonlight. In no more than a couple of minutes I had landed up safe under an oak, hardly twenty feet from the lighted living-room window.

And boy! they were really going at it. There was Pete, standing in a filthy old sweater and baggy trousers, his foot resting on a chair, his whisky glass in his hand. And there was Maria-Luisa, hands on her hips, if there were still hips under that great bulging front, tossing her head, bending forward to give point to her hisses of hatred and contempt – looking, in fact, for all the world like Anna Magnani in one of those post-war neo-realistic films. And they were really handing it out, both of them. She, louder and shriller, but he really with considerable expertise and relish. I had to hand it to him: he was holding his own, all right.

As far as I could make out, of course. Because ninety per cent of all this was going on in Italian, which is really the only language to quarrel in. They made such good use of it that I don't think I missed all that much, artistically, by not understanding: this wasn't an exercise in logic. Still, as a policeman I would dearly like to have known what it was all about. Now and then Pete would let fly with a phrase or two in English: 'You stupid bitch, you've got it wrong as usual' was one; 'Why don't you fucking learn English, then you might understand what's going on?' was another.

These were phrases principally for his own satisfaction: it was like shouting insults at a Lambretta. On and on she went, higher and higher, working herself up to a final orgasm of fury.

I noticed, while this process was at a point of screw-turning tension, that her eye was suddenly caught by her own whisky glass standing on the table, and if Pete hadn't been shouting so hard he might have noticed too. Advancing a step, she seized it in her capable kitchen hands and launched it with its contents straight at his head.

'*Bruto! Barbaro! Seduttore! Assassino!*'

It didn't need even as much as holiday Italian to understand that last one, and to wonder whether it was part of Maria-Luisa's normal repertoire of abuse, or a statement of fact or opinion.

CHAPTER 7

THE YOUNGER GENERATION

I awoke on Friday morning to the sound of policemen in the house. The sound is quite unmistakable, at least to a policeman: heavy men trying to move discreetly. I poked my head round the bedroom door: hordes of them – down in the hall, up the staircase, on the landing. Hamnet was really intending to take the place apart.

McWatters brought me breakfast on a tray, a substantial and traditional bacon-and-egg affair. He was too sensible to apologize to me for the infestation of policemen. I ate well, then I shaved and dressed and went to see what was going on. If the police were everywhere, the family was not: only Aunt Sybilla seemed to be around in the main part of the house. I expected her to be creating merry hell, but in fact she was sitting, robed and turbaned, in a small study off the hall, in pensive attitude, as if going through her Blue Period. I slipped in to have a word with Hamnet, and said I thought she was unusually quiet, given the circumstances.

'Used it all up last night,' said Tim in his phlegmatic way.

'Bad?'

'Incredible. Stood me out it was suicide, or accident, or possibly both. Said she was going to get on the phone to the Home Secretary who was a personal friend, but it turned out she was thinking of the last one but seven. But phew! I think she must be what they call a *grande dame*.'

'She'd like to think so,' I said. 'Did you get anything out of her in the end?'

'Not a thing. As far as movements were concerned, she

65

was in bed. No doubt they all were. As far as motive is concerned, she knew of nothing whatsoever. Everything was hunky-dory.'

'Hmm,' I said. 'Can you imagine this lot living together and everything being hunky-dory?'

I told him about the hypothetically missing picture, suggested his searchers should keep their eyes open, pending more details, and then I drifted off into the grounds.

My idea was that, since it was a fine day, the Squealies might be playing outside, and that I might detach one of the older ones and talk to it in an uncle-like fashion, and perhaps get things out of it that a policeman could not. A pretty fatuous idea, actually, because they did not know me as an uncle and I do look awfully like a policeman. And anyway, as Tim Hamnet found out later, they are only to be detached from one another by the strength of three men. In any case, they weren't in the grounds — I would have heard them — but I wandered around for a bit, partly for old time's sake, partly to see if anyone would spot me from the window and come out for a chat. I was just standing on the edge of a spinney down by the lake, now thick with weeds, when along came Mordred. I don't know if he had seen me from the window, but he came purposefully, all bright-eyed and bushy-tailed, neat and dapper in a tailor-made suit, and looking as if he'd just washed behind both his ears, and felt all the better for it.

'That's the tree you fell out of when you were five,' he said, pointing, 'and that's the lake you pushed me into when you were ten.'

He was full of beans, and doing none of the House of the Dead stuff. Still, none of them were.

'What a memory you have,' I replied in kind. 'I can see you're the family historian.'

'For my sins,' he said with a wry grimace. 'And until some academic job comes up in somewhere other than Qatar or Abu Dhabi. The damnable thing is, what with the general family publicity mania and now this, if I did ever get the thing finished it would probably be a best-seller. It would sell better than Pete's *magnum opus*, anyway.'

'Pete writes, does he?'

'What else?'

'What on?'

'Let him bore you with it. He'll be delighted. I hear your wife's coming tonight.'

'Now, how in God's name—?'

'Calm down. I haven't been listening in to your calls. I heard at the Marquis of Danby when I slipped down for a double Scotch last night. I can see why you don't want them here, but do bring her up for a meal, won't you?'

'If she sets her mind on it, I don't see how I can stop her,' I said gloomily. 'Short of its being one of Aunt Kate's nights.'

'She was on on Wednesday. It'll be another ten days before she's on again. With a bit of luck even you will avoid her spinach blancmange.'

'How do you stand it?' I asked.

'You mean the family in general, I take it, rather than the spinach blancmange?' He considered for a moment – really, I thought, he is quite nice, and not unintelligent. 'Well, I suppose the brute fact of the matter is that it's better than teaching. Teaching in an ordinary school, I mean. Almost anything is better than that. So long as I'm part of the great army of the unemployed I can stand it here. I'm used to Mama's little ways, and as for the rest – well, they must appear appalling to you because you've been so long away, but I find I can put up with them.'

'I hear you're looking into this notion your mother has got that a picture has disappeared from the house.'

He raised his eyebrows to heaven. 'Just what I was going to have a chat to you about last night. If it was only *one* picture, though . . .'

'She thinks a lot have gone?'

'Once she got the idea, she started thinking of things she'd known as a child — pictures, furniture, Great-Grandfather Josiah's christening spoon, God knows what. Then she'd scream they were missing, cry blue murder — and then of course she'd find them and go quiet. On the Rampage and Off the Rampage, as Joe Gargery says. Personally I don't know what to think.'

'You mean not everything's been found?'

'No, alas: we'd get some peace if it had been. Of course, stuff gets lost, furniture breaks, things get given away. But certainly there seem to be things missing.'

'What picture was it that set all this off?'

'It was a thing by Holman Hunt, called *The Rustic Wedding*. A sort of companion piece to *The Hireling Shepherd*.' I shuddered. 'Yes, indeed. I remember it dimly from childhood, and it too has greens that sear the eyeballs. Which makes it odder that it can't be found. Likewise a picture by William Allan entitled *Lord Byron Reposing in the House of a Turkish Fisherman After Having Swum the Hellespont*.'

'Christ.'

'Exactly. But if I remember it rightly, it's not something you could just tuck away somewhere.'

'But you remember it framed.'

'True. That's a point. Anyway, the fact is that these, at least, seem to be gone. Then there are Aunt Eliza's — that's another problem. Nice old thing, as I remember her, but not the most methodical of women, and her will, I hear, was a mess. Who owns the ones that are here, were there more here when she died? The fact is, I agree there should be a proper inventory made. Because the security in the house is far from impressive, and it could be that any one of us is taking them off and popping them, one by one. As my dear mother, in her nice way, made us all very much aware.'

'I gather it was suggested a professional might do the inventory.'

'Exactly. Your papa's bright contribution. Now, the

advantage of this suggestion – you don't mind if I abuse your papa, do you?'

'Be my guest.'

'Well, the advantage of this suggestion was that it *looked* as if your papa was keen to get the job done properly by insisting it be done by an outsider. And it *is* work for an expert, not for a dilettante like me. But the fact is, the expert could only deal with what is here now. He wouldn't know a thing about what *should* be here but isn't. So the proposal, to my ears, smelt just the tiniest bit fishy.'

'I see your point. Or it could have been pure mischief-making.'

'Of which your late papa knew a thing or two. Precisely. Anyway I did a bit of work on it, from the family papers and that, but by then it had all begun to die down and I dropped it. I might have done more if Uncle Lawrence had been willing to pay me, but *that* would have been out of the question, knowing the dear old phoney.'

'Are the family finances rocky?'

Mordred turned his eyes in the direction of the horizon: we could see Thornwick in the distance, and some prosperous housing estates of a private kind in between.

'I don't see how they can be, do you? It's all ours, all that. Still ours. Lawrence should be bathing in the stuff.'

'That's not quite the impression given.'

'You noticed the inclination to pinch the odd penny, did you?'

'I never expected supermarket sherry in this house.'

'Precisely. Though we're all good children and say we prefer it. If you'd like a guess at the reason for all this, I'd say it's because he hasn't been able to bring himself to make the house and all the doings over to Pete.'

'Of course!' I said. 'So the death duties—'

'Will be colossal. The only time I ever remember the subject coming up, he muttered: "Heed the Bard. Remember King Lear." I suppose he foresees himself being turned out into a Corporation old people's home – our modern equivalent of the heath. I imagine he's penny-pinching in anticipation of death duties – though that doesn't quite make sense either, unless he's salting it away somewhere secret. The fact is, Uncle Lawrence is only passing fond of Peter, but he absolutely dotes on the Squealies.'

'So I noticed. He's totally senile, I take it.'

'Only so-so. He can tell a hawk from a handsaw when the wind's southerly. Anyway, the fact is, it could be Lawrence putting the pictures up for sale, as is his perfect right.'

'And being too embarrassed to say?'

'Exactly. So what you've got here is either a fine old can of worms, or conceivably a storm in a teacup.'

'Had all this caused much trouble – for example, between my father and Uncle Lawrence?'

'Not that I noticed. There was no more than the normal quota of sniping, heavy ironies, double-edged innuendoes and so on – the usual currency of communication in this house.'

We had been walking through the golden trees, under falling leaves, and we now arrived back at the lawn behind the house. Mordred paused in the shade of a tree.

'See that window in the Elizabethan wing?' he said. 'That's Peter's sitting-room.'

'I know. I spied on him last night. I saw Maria-Luisa clock him with a whisky glass.'

'Good for her. Now, in that window is my cousin – our cousin – Pete. And I bet you anything you like that if you walk across this lawn alone he will call you in and pump you for all you're worth.'

'How do you know?'

'I know Cousin Pete. Inheritor of Harpenden House, and future head of the Trethowan family.'

He started off in the direction of the Florentine wing, but I caught his arm and kept him a moment longer in the shadow.

70

'Morrie – if my wife comes here, can I rely on you?'

'What? To see they all behave themselves?'

'No – to make sure they don't. I want her to see them at their worst. I couldn't bear a big reconciliation, with family visits in the summer hols.'

'I'll do my best, but I should hardly think it will be necessary. With nerves all tensed up as they are now, anything can happen.'

With which prophecy of ferment Morrie trotted off happily in the direction of the Florentine wing – his tie as straight as when he had emerged, his shoes as spick and dust-free. There are some men nature can't touch.

But he was dead right about Pete. Because I was just strolling, oh so casual, in the direction of the main block, when he appeared in his sitting-room window.

'Oh, I say, Perry—' I turned coolly. 'I say, are you at leisure, or on the beat, as it were?'

'Pretty much at leisure,' I said.

'Could I have a word with you, old man? Nothing frightfully important, but—'

I strolled over to him. 'But—?'

'But . . . I'd just like a word,' he concluded feebly. He was in that damn denim suit again, which made him look ten years older than his real age. Have you noticed it's only aging phoneys who wear denim suits? Well, it is, exclusively. This phoney had a bad bruise over his left eye, and I asked with concern: 'Been in an accident?'

'My marriage is one long accident,' said Pete gloomily. The sound of the Squealies, playfully scalping each other several floors up, lent point to his remark. 'I say, I'll come round to the side door and let you in.'

'Don't bother,' I said, easing myself up on to the window ledge and swivelling my legs round into the room.

'Maria-Luisa's all het up about security. Every door locked, and bolts on the one through to the main house. Crazy bitch. That's what comes of being born and bred among the Mafia.'

Peter and Maria-Luisa's sitting-room was a fairly

comfortable affair, with a lot of 'thirties furniture retrieved from the main house, or perhaps left in this wing by Aunt Eliza. There was no great impress of personality on the room, however, unless it was the untidy scattering of books and papers around the place, which could have been strewn for my benefit.

'Excuse the mess,' said Peter perfunctorily. 'This is the overflow from my study.'

'I hear you write,' I said. (I would never have dreamt, by the way, of giving him an opening like that if it wasn't that I knew I had to find out something about him and his life.)

'Mmmm,' said Peter. 'At the moment I'm reviewing. A load of sex books, for the *New Spectator*.' He gestured towards the sofa, where lay a disorder of books, among them such surefire American best-sellers as *Sex and the Stock-Market* by Theodore S. Rosenheim and *Is There Sex After Death?* by Dr Philip Krumm-Kumfitt.

'I'm pretty much the *New Spectator*'s sex man these days,' said Peter contentedly.

'Really?' (Well, you think of a reply to that.)

'What with that and the novel, I've got my hands full,' he went on, with killing casualness.

'Novel?' I said, playing my part like a ventriloquist's dummy.

'Ye-e-es,' said Peter, as if reluctant to speak of it, but since I'd brought the topic up . . . 'A really big one, something on the scale of the old three-volume affairs.'

'Have you got far with it?'

'Oh, so-so.' He gestured with his hands, as if to indicate a thick pile. 'I write reams and discard a lot. Discard the whole time. I'm a perfectionist.'

'What . . . sort of thing is it?'

'Well, you know, novels today are all niminy-piminy little affairs, written by housewives between the nappy-changes, or academics in their summer hols. God! British novels these days are so unambitious! They're positively anaemic.'

'Yours will have blood, will it?'

'I see it as a sort of sexual odyssey, if you see what I mean, combined . . . com*bined* with an enormous social conspectus, a sort of diagnosis of current social ills, get what I mean? *Bleak House* was the model I had in mind.'

'I should have thought *Nightmare Abbey* might be a more appropriate model for someone living at Harpenden,' I said.

He looked at me closely. 'You don't like us very much, do you, Perry?'

I shrugged my shoulders. 'I only meant this house can't be the most peaceful place for a writer to work in.'

Peter wagged a fat finger at me. 'It's having the leisure that counts, it's not being a part-time writer. It's *only* the old upper classes – the *rem*nants of the upper classes – that have the *time* to conceive anything really *big* these days. Look at your father—'

'He never conceived anything bigger than a musical fart in his whole life,' I protested.

'Well, he was a bit different,' Pete admitted. 'What I meant was, he had *leisure*. He could *wait* on inspiration.'

'He certainly waited,' I agreed. 'What was it you wanted to talk to me about, Pete?'

This chat was not going very well, and I wasn't helping it to go any better. Wasn't I supposed to be worming my way into their confidences? Hearing their artless, gushing confessions? I was hardly going to succeed in that if I made it so abundantly plain I couldn't stand any manjack of them. And my direct question had very obviously embarrassed Pete, who had clearly intended to come round to this topic via several B-roads, public footpaths and back alleys.

'I just wondered . . .' he muttered, '. . . you know . . . how the police were . . . regarding the case. How it was going . . . Whether they were getting any leads.'

'You'll no doubt have a chance to ask Superintendent Hamnet that yourself before long.'

'Well, yes, that's partly the point . . . You're the expert,

73

Perry. I was wondering how to approach that . . . interview. Wondering what line I should take.'

I raised my eyebrows. This really took the biscuit. What could one do but take refuge in cliché? 'What can you expect me to say but that you should tell the truth?'

'Oh, come off it, Perry. Don't be so bloody Dixon of Dock Green. There's truth and truth. Now, take this suggestion that one of my kids may have done it.'

'Ah! Whose suggestion is that?'

'Oh, it's . . . going around. Now, what line am I supposed to take on that, for example?'

He grinned, as if somehow he'd made a point I was incapable of seeing. 'You don't have to take any line,' I said, exasperated. 'All he'll want to know is whether it could have happened. Could they have got out of this wing, for example?'

'We *usually* lock them in their bedrooms,' said Peter. 'On the other hand, we sometimes forget.'

'Did you forget the night before last?'

'How should I remember? It was chaos that night. The suggestion hadn't come up then.'

'And Maria-Luisa? Does she remember?'

'Oh, she'll swear herself black and blue it was locked. She'd do that if everyone else had heard them rampaging through the house. Perjury isn't a crime in Sicily: it's a family duty.'

'There probably wouldn't be any question of perjury. The case could hardly come to court. They're obviously too young to know what they're doing.'

'That's rather what I thought,' said Pete speculatively.

'Unless, of course,' I proceeded weightily, 'someone put them up to it.'

Pete darted a sharp glance at me. 'Oh, come off it. You've seen my kids. Can you imagine them doing something they'd been put up to?'

I spread out my hands. 'Perhaps. If the idea appealed to them. If they thought it was fun. It might depend on their relationship with whoever it was.'

74

'Meaning me or Maria-Luisa, no doubt. Hmmm. Yes, well I can see there are dangers in that line.'

'Why,' I asked nastily, 'are you trying to take a line? What are you trying to cover up?'

'I'm not trying to cover anything up, I'm just trying to get the whole silly business over and done with.' He bent forward in his chair opposite me, in a gesture of intimacy I shrank back from. 'Look, Perry: you know what your father was. He was an insignificant little troublemaker without an ounce of talent. I'm not particularly happy he's been done in,' (he said this rather quickly, as if he realized he was laying himself open) 'but I'm not going to pretend I care a button either. Even if it was, say, McWatters or Mrs Mac. They do a good job, and we couldn't cope if we lost them. If admitting one of the kids might have done it – and they might have – will get us back to normal so that I can get on with some work, then so be it. I still might, if you forget this daft idea they might have been put up to it, and if I can knock some sense into their silly cow of a mother. You know us, Perry. You can't expect any conventional law and order stuff in this house.'

'Even if it means leaving a murderer at large among you?'

'I can take care of myself,' he said, puffing out some flab.

'Well,' I said, getting up, 'you're obviously going to take your own way, whatever I advise. But I'll tell you one thing: if it was one of your children, doing it in a spirit of youthful fun, you can be pretty sure Hamnet will find it out.'

'Will he interview them?' said Pete admiringly. 'Christ, I wouldn't be in his shoes.'

'Obviously he'll have to, since this has come up. I'm sure he'll know the best way to deal with them.'

Peter narrowed his eyes: 'What do you mean by that? I know you police: he'll try and bully them into saying one of us put them up to it. I tell you, if he lays a finger on one of them, I'll get my lawyer on to him and have him up for assault.'

'Good to know you think the law has its uses,' I said, vaulting out of the window.

And I walked back to the main block, happily chewing over the notion that Pete was willing to dub one of his own kids in, if it would win him a bit of peace and quiet. Which no doubt was what the quarrel was about last night. All things considered, I thought my cousin Pete was as nasty a specimen of humanity as I had met in years of treating with the criminal classes, and it was good to know that the Trethowan estates were to go to such a worthy inheritor.

CHAPTER 8

LUNCH WITH UNCLE LAWRENCE

When I went back into the house, Aunt Sybilla called me into the dark little study off the entrance hall, once, I believe, my grandfather's business room where he dealt with all the estate accounts, now a rather unattractive writing-room. I doubted whether much writing went on there as a general rule, and was quite sure Aunt Sybilla had spent the morning in it because it gave her a good view on to the hall, and hence on to the comings and goings in the house as a whole. Something seemed to have happened to put her into a better humour than when I saw her earlier.

'Well, Peregrine, I gave all possible help last night to your nice friend from the Force.'

When Aunt Sybilla lies, she does so with total conviction, and when she is found out lying she can summon up a truly Pecksniffian self-righteous outrage.

'I'm sure he's grateful,' I said.

'I hope so. Have you seen the papers today?'

'No,' I shuddered. So this was the cause of the beam of sunlight that had brightened her morning.

'Well, I got on to my friends in Fleet Street. Not all of them. Some of them had died!' She said this in a tone of affront, as if they had deserted their posts. 'As a result, there's only a silly little piece in the *Grub*. But otherwise we've been done proud! They've given us a really good spread!'

'Aunt Sybilla, do you think—?'

'I shall give them further *dribbles* of information from time to time. And, of course, exclusive interviews when it's over and the monster is caught. *Who* can it be, do you think, Perry? *Who* could wish to kill your father? A man without an enemy in the world. A verray parfit gentil knight, or the younger brother of one, at any rate.'

'I'm afraid, Aunt Sybilla, you should face up to the fact that it's most likely to have been someone in this house.'

'Impossible! Unless it was a Squealy. I do think that's a definite possibility. If it was, he'd be packed off to a Reformatory, wouldn't he?' Her face expressed delighted anticipation, but then it fell again. 'Not that it would make much difference. They keep coming all the time.'

'Did you want me for anything, Aunt Sybilla?'

'Did I what? Oh, yes. I've told Mrs McWatters that you will lunch with Lawrence. He's in good form today, thank heavens, so you should seize the chance. A good head-to-head, as the French say. Of course, we'd love to have had you ourselves. Mordred said especially to ask you because he really finds you quite interesting, but . . .'

'Thank you,' I said. 'I'm looking forward to a talk with Uncle.'

'Exactly. Get in while the going's good. Because tomorrow he could have Gone Off, as it were.'

So that was that. I was doomed to lunch with the famous Survivor of the Trenches. (I never found out, by the way, whether my Uncle Lawrence ever did any actual fighting in the First World War, or whether he so much as saw a trench. He was not eighteen until July 1918, and he certainly didn't lie about his age to get in early. Of course one could get killed as easily in the last days of the war as in the first, as Wilfred Owen found out, but malicious family rumour, fostered by my father, suggested that Lawrence's closest view of the war, like Hemingway's, was from the front end of a stretcher while serving in the Ambulance Corps. It was on leave in December 1918, in the euphoria of peace, that Lawrence met and married his first wife, a chorus girl.)

I went along to have a bit of a natter with Tim Hamnet. He had been interviewing Aunt Kate, and looked dazed. I told him about the paintings, and he sent a message through to his men to keep their eyes open for any rustic scene in liver-congealing greens, and any picture with Turkish overtones. We discussed the Squealy idea, which seemed to possess such attractions for the various adult occupants of the house: we weren't really sold on the notion; though, as Tim said, there was something about the method of the murder which suggested a naughty child. To fill in the half-hour until lunch I went off and glanced at the papers. And then wished I hadn't. FAMOUS FAMILY'S TORTURE CHAMBER shrieked one. TORTURE HORROR IN STATELY HOME yelled another. The stories were in kind, and I began to get rather angry until I suddenly decided that really you couldn't blame journalists: when they blew something up from nothing and persecuted inoffensive citizens – that's when you should get angry. But this was hardly nothing, and it had been handed to them on a plate by a publicity-crazed Sybilla. One would have to be a saint not to rub one's hands a bit at a story like that, and Fleet Street seldom runs to saints.

Lunch was simple, mostly salad, and it was served by Mrs McWatters.

'McWatters is in with the policemen, helping with Mrs Trethowan,' she explained, and I couldn't remotely think what she meant.

She was a stern-faced, rigid woman, the sort who look as if they go around singing 'Their land brought forth frogs' under their breath all day. I wondered how someone whose soul seemed to have been entered by the iron of

Presbyterianism could bear to live day by day in the vicinity of the Trethowans.

Uncle Lawrence was in a little motorized chair, and he got himself into the room and up to the head of the table with a good deal of dexterity. On his good days he could easily do without Kate, which was worth remembering. On ground-floor level, anyway, he was as mobile as if he had the use of his legs. At least now he knew who I was, and he greeted me expansively.

'Ah, Perry, m'boy. How are things? Sorry I wasn't at m'best yesterday. These things happen at my age, y'know. They looking after you all right?'

'Very well indeed, thank you.'

'You'll have to come more often, now your father's gone, eh? See to – what's her name? – Cristobel, now she's on her own. I suppose she gets the loot, eh?'

'I sincerely hope so, if there is any.'

'What? If there is any? 'Course there is. Rolling. Must be. What did he have to spend it on, eh?'

'Do-it-yourself strappado machines,' I suggested.

Lawrence roared with laughter. 'Dear me. Most unseemly. Brother's going, and all that. Still. When you think of it: those that live by the sword shall perish by the sword, what? eh? Same principle.'

There was a dreadful cheeriness about Uncle Lawrence's discussion of my father's death that was hardly decent. After all, he could scarcely have disliked him as much as I did, otherwise he'd have booted him out of the house long ago. In the intervals of his wheezy chuckles he was tucking heartily into his meal. Salad wasn't the easiest thing for a man partly paralyzed by a stroke to eat: he intently got a few bits of this and that on to his fork, then effortfully raised it to his mouth, the last few inches – past his oh-so-Bohemian cravat – being particularly painful. Still, he managed, and chatted on in his old way the meanwhile.

'Have any contact with y'father, Perry, after you left?'

'None whatsoever.'

'No reconciliation, eh? What was the trouble?'

'I believe he objected to my calling him a mediocrity.'

This delighted Lawrence. 'Seriously? How splendid! Well, he wasn't much, was he? Dried-out little talent, that's about all you could call it. You'd've thought setting Swinburne might have inspired him, eh? chap like that. But it didn't. At the end there was even less. It just trickled away and he wrote nothing. Too busy with his infernal machines, what?'

'Did he have any – what shall I say? – accomplices in his special tastes? I mean—' this was horribly awkward – 'he didn't pay people to beat him, or anything?'

Lawrence guffawed again. 'No, he was essentially a man of solitary vices.' But he thought, and I think he perceived that the drift of my question might have led the search away from the occupants of Harpenden. 'Mind you, I don't know what he did when he went to London. You can get all sorts of people to do things for you there, what? – sort of thing you wouldn't want to ask one of the gardeners to do. Soho's still what it was, eh? And then there's the little man who made his machines.'

'Did he come here?'

'Think so. Organized the installation and all that, don't you know. Never saw him m'self.'

'Did he go to London often?'

'Not so much in recent years. Too damned expensive. Still, I imagine he still had contacts.'

'You didn't have any quarrel with him yourself?'

'Quarrel? No. Didn't like the man. Couldn't be bothered to quarrel with him.'

'You didn't think he'd been taking pictures and selling them?'

'That damnfool idea of Sybilla's? No – nothing in it. Silly buzzard gets these bees in her bonnet. Not that there's not some valuable stuff in the house.' He fumbled stiffly in his pockets. 'Got a letter today. Some place or other in America. Philadelphia, that's it. Some damn woman writing. Setting up some kind of museum of female art. Ever heard such nonsense, eh? Lot of rubbish they'll have, eh? But they want some of Eliza's stuff. Got one already, want more. Hmm. Think I'll hold out on them for a bit. Make 'em more eager. They can't have much stuff as good as hers.'

I had looked into Germaine Greer's book on women painters and their wrongs, and remembering the dire assemblage of illustrations I could only agree. I didn't know which would be worse, the collection of paintings, or the sort of person who would go and see it. Still, it was all rather interesting. I noted that Lawrence was far from ruling out the idea of selling.

'There seems to be some idea going round,' I said casually, 'that one of Peter's children might have cut the cord – completely in play, of course.'

That really set Uncle Lawrence off. Obviously no one had dared broach the idea to him before.

'What? Whose idea was that? Absolute poppycock. Never heard such bilge in m'life. Little darlings! Have you ever seen such little sweetlings? Wouldn't enter their heads, not for a moment. They like a bit of fun and games, but they'd never do a thing like that. You stamp firmly on any talk you hear. Absolute balderdash.'

'I'm not madly keen on the idea myself,' I said calmly.

But Lawrence had clearly been upset, and now began to toy fretfully with his ice-cream. He seemed to be getting tired, because there was little more in the way of conversation to be got out of him, and he sat there muttering 'poppycock' and 'nasty nonsense' and things of that kind, making me feel the most utter louse even for mentioning it.

Luckily, after a bit Mrs McWatters appeared and came over to whisper in my ear: 'The Inspector says, they've found the scissors, sir.'

'What? Speak up! No secrets here. What's that you're saying?' bellowed Uncle Lawrence.

'The Inspector,' said Mrs McWatters in a deep Clara-Butt-exhorting-Britain-to-rule-the-waves voice, 'said to tell Mr Peregrine that the scissors have been found.'

'Scissors? What does he want scissors for? I could have lent them a pair of scissors if they'd asked,' said Uncle Lawrence.

CHAPTER 9

PAPA'S PAPERS

The finding of the scissors that had cut the thread of my papa's destiny raised my spirits no end. It seemed to suggest – quite irrationally – that at last we might be getting somewhere, that before long there might be an end to this nightmare, and I might shake the dust of Harpenden House off my feet and head back to real life. Perhaps I wouldn't even stay for the funeral: no one had asked me to it, after all, and I had only come under the sternest call of duty. Almost without realizing it, I burst into song as I made my way through the hall and down the corridor to the Gothic wing:

> ' "Come down and redeem us from virtue,
> Our Lady of Pain." '

'Christ Almighty,' said Tim Hamnet, meeting me at the door of our wing. 'What's that?'

'A section of my father's masterwork, the song-cycle *Dolores*,' I said. 'To words by Swinburne. It should be sung by a tenor, but it doesn't make it sound any better. Come on, Tim, spill the beans. Where?'

'Stuffed down the side of a flowerpot. The earth was only slightly disturbed – bit of luck our chap noticed it. A London copper probably wouldn't have. I'll show you.' He led the way back to the hall, and then down the corridor leading (past numberless small, dark and totally useless rooms) to the Florentine wing. On an old, low occasional table, was a pot containing the plant known as mother-in-law's tongue. I raised the bladelike leaves gently, and looked at the place where the scissors had been pushed down.

'Hmm. Interesting. What sort were they?'

'Largish pair of nail-scissors. Sharp — very good quality — German-made. You don't get that class of article from Sheffield these days. McWatters says they belonged in one of the downstairs bathrooms. I've sent them off to the boffins, but it's pretty obvious they did the job, isn't it?'

'For the moment I can't think of a hundred and one other reasons for stuffing a pair of nail-scissors down a flowerpot,' I said. 'Well, we're a step or so for'arder. We can certainly knock on the head the idea that it was one of the Squealies having a bit of childish fun. They'd just have dropped the scissors, or put them back where they found them.'

'Whereas anyone else—?'

'Would, I guess, have seen that the scissors, if they belonged to the house, and if the forensic bods could prove that they cut the cord, would have brought the murder home irrevocably to one of the inhabitants. Or at the very best to someone who knew the house well.'

'Your family have many friends these days, Perry?'

'Friends in the area? I don't get that impression. They don't seem to have been deluged by phone-calls of sympathy. I'm not surprised. Can you imagine old Jack 'Obbs from the village tottering up to have a natter about his rheumatiz with one of this lot? Of course, the McWatterses may have friends.'

'Remarkable chap, that. Engaging, too.'

'What on earth was he with you at lunchtime for? His better half — who is *not* engaging — said something about Mrs Trethowan. Sybilla calls herself Miss Trethowan these days, so I suppose she must have meant Maria-Luisa?'

'Yes. He was translating.'

'He was *what*?'

'Translating. Unorthodox, but since they didn't seem to be able to get anybody locally, and thinking of the time it would take to get someone from London, I decided to take the risk. She obviously had enough English to protest if he misrepresented what she said. Just won't speak it, the lazy bitch.'

'And how come the Admirable Crichton is fluent in gutter Italian?'

'War service, so he said.'

I calculated. 'The war's been over thirty-five years or so. That makes McWatters at least fifty-five. I'd have put him five or ten years younger myself, but he is sort of ageless. The quiet, withdrawn type that time doesn't line. Still, his wife looks all of mid-fifty, so I suppose it's probably true. Interesting in the circumstances, I must say. Did you get anything out of Maria-Luisa?'

'Protestations of the innocence of her infants, swearings to God and the Holy Virgin that they were locked in, maledictions – I learned the word *maledetto* without any trouble – on those who tried to pin such an atrocious crime on her innocent angels. Nothing of any substance, in other words.'

'Predictable, I suppose. Still, a bit more engaging than their ghastly father, whose first thought was to shop them for the crime.'

'Doing anything this afternoon, Perry?' said Tim. 'If not, I've got a job for you.'

'Interviewing the Squealies or something dangerous like that, I suppose? I think you should call in the Specials.'

'Actually, I'm doing that myself, with assistance. No, I'd like you to go upstairs into your father's quarters and go through all his papers and things. You know your way around up there, know where he kept all his stuff, I imagine, and it's possible you might come across something we might pass over.'

'I suppose I could. What am I looking for?'

'Well, obviously anything that could have caused trouble

86

between your father and the family. Money, those pictures, anything of that sort. And possibly anything connected with his nasty little sexual practices. The person who made the machines, any pals with similar tastes — I'd like to know about them. Do you think he had contacts with others of his kind?'

'For all I know they held a von Sacher-Masoch memorial dinner once a year at the Savoy,' I said. 'Or else they got my Aunt Kate to cook one for them. Actually, that's what put me in mind of that song . . .'

'What song?'

' "When thy lips had such lovers to flatter;
    When the city lay red from thy rods," '

I bellowed.

'Don't do that, Perry, please.'

'That song-cycle *Dolores*. I wonder whether it wasn't some sort of covert announcement — of his tastes, I mean, and an appeal to others of his kind to make contact. It makes it pretty bloody obvious. On the other hand, Uncle Lawrence said not: implied it was very much a solitary thing with my papa.'

'Well, keep it in mind while you're looking around, eh, Perry?'

And so I climbed the stairs and at last went back to my childhood home. I can't describe the sensations I had: for minutes on end I just pushed open doors and wandered through the old rooms — so well remembered, and hardly changed. The drawing-room, my mother's little sitting-room, my father's library and study, my cosy round bedroom in the turret, and Cristobel's room just beside it. I imagine everybody going home after a long time away feels a bit like me. But I suppose most of them have a lot of happy memories. It wasn't that I had none; on the other hand, it wasn't those that came back to me. The oddest thing of all was that, though my father and Cristobel had lived here alone for fifteen years, it wasn't their presence I felt here at all: it was my mother's, investing every room with memories: I came upon her as I turned corners, I saw her back as she sat at her writing-desk, I imagined her lying on the sofa with a rug over her, I heard her thin voice calling to me. My mother – whom I'd barely thought of twice a year since I'd grown up and left home.

I think my mother was a sort of survivor, one of a species that could not fend for itself in the modern world but had clung precariously on in tiny numbers. I suppose you'd call her well born: she came of a very old Cumberland family with a splendid pedigree and lots of in-breeding. My mother drifted through life – thin, Roman-nosed, kind and remote – with not a thought of how to grapple with the realities or fight battles for herself. Things were done for one, weren't they? It was an odd world she lived in – one where she had family, 'birth', a place in society, appointed duties, the respect of the peasantry. Even in Jane Austen's time such people ought to have known the world was changing; my mother never seemed to learn. My father proposed. She was thirty and unmarried. Her family was hard up, as an old family always is that has not sent representatives into the big worlds of banking and commerce and industry. They told her she should accept, and she accepted, drifting into marriage as she had drifted into everything else she had done in life.

I don't suppose she was marked down for happiness, but in some other marriage, or in respectable spinsterhood, she might have got through life with some dignity and contentment. My picture of her is of sickness, and bewilderment, and a sort of helpless and impractical love for me and Cristobel. She was an ailing body, probably from my birth, or even before. I remember in the 'fifties her taking long cruises for her health – cruises to the West Indies, cruises round the world, in the belief that what she needed was sun and change. Nothing helped. She lay, almost throughout my childhood, on the sofa in her little sitting-room, flickering, angular, sad.

I remember her taking me to her one day and telling me that if anything happened to her – as if I didn't know, at ten, exactly what was going to happen to her – I was to look after my small sister. It came to me now with a pang that I hadn't made much of a fist of it. I'd walked out on the job.

The memories got on top of me. To get away from them I went through into my father's study, a room where I never remember my mother going. It was the room with fewest personal associations for me, too: not a place we were called into often, or to which we went of our own accord, though it opened out into the little library, where I spent many hours. Dominating the room, on the wall that got most sunlight, was a painting by Salvador Dali, a picture of various things melting into various other things, a purchase of Aunt Eliza's in the 'twenties: it was vaguely nasty, but it went with the room. Also dominant was the grand piano over by the leaded windows, where my father would go and try over the inspirations that crowded in on him. It was very dusty. I tried it and it was out of tune. On the table nearby was a pile of music, including a few of my father's own compositions in manuscript. I took up the Jubilee *Hymn of Tribute*, written in my father's thin, quavery musical notation: a page of it looked like the death-throes of a consumptive spider. It was a setting of some bilge by John Masefield, and I wondered whether it had in fact been written for the 1935 Jubilee, and resurrected for the more recent one. I moved over to the desk.

In spite of his apparent openness about his amusing little vices, my father was in many ways a secretive man: he certainly didn't 'give himself' (thank God) to his family, nor, I imagine, to his friends. On the other hands, he was meticulous in his habits, and I found evidence in the desk that my Uncle Lawrence's condition of intermittent senility had frightened him and made him take precautions. For example, he left a notebook labelled 'Apparatus', with precise details of what had been ordered for his games room, and how much had been paid for it. It was clear that almost all the equipment had been devised and constructed by one Ramsay Percival, of 118 Reform Street, Newcastle. I went through the book, marvelling at the scrupulous recording of the progress of the various machines, often with little diagrams. He had noted down the sums paid to Percival – 'to prevent fraud in the event of my death or incapacity'. I totted up the various amounts relating to the strappado: it came to about the cost of a second-hand Mini. Well, I suppose we all have our forms of self-torment. The rack, unfinished, looked as if it would have cost considerably more.

The stubs of my father's cheque-book also bore the name of Percival pretty frequently, but otherwise were unrevealing. Mostly they were to Cristobel, presumably for housekeeping purposes. There was nothing else around on the desk that was at all personal – no blotters with letters that could be read in reverse, no letters *to* him either (but who would write?). I tried the drawers: little clipped bundles of bills, unrevealing except for some from Soho bookshops and a receipt from a theatrical costumier (for the tights, no doubt).

In the bottom drawer was my mother's will. I thought of it fondly: it had left everything to be divided equally between Cristobel and me, and what it came to was about a thousand pounds each. It's rather a neither-here-nor-there kind of sum, but I thought of it with gratitude, because it had tided me over when I slammed out of the house, before I got myself into the army, and it had paid for a fortnight's honeymoon in Portugal, more or less. It hadn't gone astray, my mother's thousand. I took a bet with myself that Cristobel had just saved hers – a pretty lunatic procedure these days, but she is the sort that tries to be farsighted and falls into a gravel pit whilst being so.

As I opened by mother's will, a little slip of paper fell out – the sort of slip that you tear off a pad and write messages to yourself on. It just said, in my father's anaemic script: 'Letter WOAF'. I puzzled over it for a bit. No doubt one of his hedges against mental decay, but what did it mean? Had it just fallen into my mother's will, or did it for some reason belong there? There was nothing about a letter in the will itself, which was simple and touching in its references to Cristobel and me, and did not mention my father at all. And what on earth were the initials? It looked like some female branch of the armed services, but if so I'd never heard of it.

I got up and shook myself: how my mother seemed to be coming back to me, like a courteously reproachful ghost, getting a gentle revenge for all those years when I'd shoved her to the back of my mind. It was my father that was my business, though. I walked over to the book-cases in the study. There were the tall shelves with his favourite scores: wispy composers like Fauré, Poulenc and Hugo Wolf. There were the books of musical reference. And then there was the case devoted to his own special kink: much loved works like *Salammbô*, *Justine* and (oddly in such company) various novels by Harrison Ainsworth. Then there were two shelves of those distasteful pseudo-scientific studies of torture which had haunted my child-hood, shoulder to shoulder with several gloating studies of all varieties of corporal infliction. I flicked through the torture books and found the fullest possible description of strappado: it was much-thumbed, and had clearly formed the basis for the streamlined, motorized version downstairs. I put the book aside to show Tim Hamnet.

I felt unclean. That sounds like a piece of evidence given by a respectable lady witness to one of the Whitehouse commissions on porn, but it's exactly how I felt. I wanted to get out of that room, and I pushed open the door to the library and went quickly through. It was dark and musty and unused. Perhaps like the chapel it had outlived its day, had now only the stale whiff of an old habit, discontinued. I had spent many happy hours here in childhood – when I was a small child, that is, in the days before the apple-stealing and the sportiness and the general anti-Trethowan rumbustiousness. When I was small my mother worried about me – roaming around, climbing trees and fells, playing with the rough village boys. She liked me to be where she could call me, from her sofa. When she saw I was substantially there, she would fade away quite happily again into the chintzy background, and I could go off – to sit, as often as not, in this library and read. That's the paradise of children with too much time on their hands. I read books much too old for me (or so librarians would say, but how can they have been too old for me if I enjoyed them?). I read *Oliver Twist* and *Nicholas Nickleby* – I always loved the Dotheboys Hall scenes, till my father put me off them by reading them aloud. I suppose I sensed the relish. I read *Jane Eyre* and *The Mill on the Floss*, and I even read bits of books ridiculously old for me: *The Ordeal of Richard Feverel*, and *The Way Of All Flesh*. Here they all were, in their musty, dull bindings: heavy, three-volume editions that I had difficulty heaving off the shelves and propping up on my small lap. Here was my absolute favourite of all: *Dombey and Son*. Why had I loved that so much? There never was a boy less like Paul Dombey than I was. I suppose it was just the vague general resemblance which gave it its special relevance: the boy and his sister, the antipathetic father, the frail, distant mother floating gradually into eternity at the end of the first chapter.

My mother . . .

I sat there, with all my thoughts, and impressions, and the ideas that danced and jeered and tantalized by refusing to come forward. Only connect . . . I had an odd feeling that I had connected momentarily, and it had flown from my mind. I pulled myself together. It must be an illusion. In fact, I had spent the whole afternoon and early evening wallowing in my past, and not at all doing what I was supposed to do. Still, I doubted if there was much here to discover that I had missed. I made a quick decision. I would go down and report to Tim Hamnet, and then I would go and tell the family (God! what an awful

expression! As if they were mine!). I would go and tell
the Trethowans that I would not be dining tonight. Then
I would hijack a police car – the place was crawling with
them – and go off to the village and spend the evening and
night with Daniel and Jan. Since they had come, I might
as well take advantage of it. I looked at my watch. Half
past six. They could even have arrived by now.

Tim was still on the ground floor, and boy! was he
looking frazzled. His collar and tie were askew, and there
were big, dark blue sweat marks under his armpits.

'Sweet little kiddies, aren't they?' I said. 'Talk about
trailing clouds of glory . . .'

'God! Don't talk to me about them, Perry.'

'How did it go? Did you talk to them all together?'

'Do I look crazy? I sent three men to prise them apart,
and a fourth to cope with their mother. I saw them one by
one, and only the three eldest. Frankly, I couldn't take
any more.'

'What did they do?'

'Screamed abuse, ran at me and started scratching
my face, yelled blue murder and started pounding on the
door.'

'Is there a magic recipe for dealing with them?'

'I'd *like* to slaughter the lot of them.'

'Ah, the Herod approach. Not allowed in the Book of
Rules, unfortunately. What did you actually do?'

'Made friends, cajoled, flattered, bribed, threatened,
bullied – pretty much in that order.'

'And what did you get out of them?'

'Nothing. They had never done such a thing, never
thought about it (but wish they had), were locked in their
bedrooms all night, didn't know Great-Uncle was dead
until the morning, and would I tell them all the details?
That was the oldest, and actually he asked for the details
first: it was only by promising them I got the rest out
of him.'

'Do you believe them?'

'Don't altogether know. Their stories agree.'

'Good sign, or bad?'

'With that lot I'd be inclined to say good. I think if anyone had tried to spoonfeed a story to them, it would have had the opposite to the desired effect. What about you, Perry? Anything of interest?'

'Meagre,' I said. I showed him the notebook about the various torture machines, the book with the description of strappado, the meaningless slip of paper from the will – and that was about it. I really felt ashamed it was so meagre. We nattered things through for a bit, and then I told him in no uncertain terms I was going off duty. I don't think he liked that, but I laid down the law (so to speak) to him: since I was down here quite unofficially, there was no way he could hold me to a twenty-four hour working day.

My spirits heightened perceptibly as I left the Gothic wing. At least for a night I was going to get out of this hell-hole, this Victorian gaol. I nearly sang as I strode across the hall – something nice, not *Dolores*. I'd drive to the village, and I'd have Jan and Daniel in my arms, and I'd play games with Daniel until his bedtime, and then we'd have a pint or two together in the Saloon and take whatever was offering in the way of food at the Marquis, and after that . . .

I opened the door to the drawing-room. There they all were, assembled for sherry. There was Sybilla, in her usual flimsy drapes, with Mordred standing beside her. There was Lawrence, with Kate at attention by his chair. And there was Cristobel, very white and all too obviously trying to be brave.

And there, looking ravishingly pretty, holding a sherry glass and talking animatedly, for all the world as if she were at home, was Jan. And clutching shyly to her skirts was Daniel.

'Ah, do you know each other?' said Uncle Lawrence.

CHAPTER 10

FAMILY AT WAR

Now the fact is, I had prepared in my mind all sorts
of injunctions and prohibitions for Jan as to how to behave
when she finally came face to face with the awful shock
of my family. Such as not admitting for a moment to
the slightest twinge of interest in anything artistic or
cultural: not even such things as singing in choirs, or
Adult Ed. courses in batik. I had it all worked out: say
you're doing Arabic to help oppressed Middle-Eastern
shop-lifters in London, or to write a book on conditions
in the modern harem that will cause the Saudi-Arabians
to break off diplomatic relations – anything except an
interest in tenth-century love poetry. Give the Trethowans
an inch and they claim four thousand acres and build a
mansion on it: admit to the merest murmuring of an
aesthetic sense and they rope you in on the family act,
claim you as a spiritual soul-mate, invite you to participate
in poetry readings with them.

And it was all thrown away. For here was Jan swilling
good sherry (I could see the bottle) with them, and talking – if my ears did not deceive me – about Harrison
Birtwistle or some such OK name. Nevertheless, I folded
her and Daniel in my arms, because after all it wasn't
their fault they hadn't had the benefit of my good advice.
While I was about it, I kissed Cristobel too, who was
looking wan but serviceable and obviously benefiting from
the Guiding instinct to keep hitting the trail.

'What a lovely surprise for you, Perry,' cooed Aunt

Sybilla. 'As soon as Mordred told me they were coming I knew you'd want to see them as soon as possible, and I sent down a little missive to the Marquis of Danby.'

Since she obviously imagined I'd be delighted, I muttered my thanks, and shot Morrie the sort of glance a schoolboy gives the class sneak.

'It's awfully nice, Peregrine,' pursued Sybilla, 'that you at least *married* a truly spiritual person – I mean *spirituelle*. Alas, that is *not* always the case in our family. For example, Lawrence's wives—'

Uncle Lawrence burst out into a shout of complacent laughter: 'Sluts! What I wanted. What I got. Sluts!'

'Yes, well . . . And dear Maria-Luisa, though an *excellent* mother as far as quantity is concerned, does just a teeny bit lack *esprit*. But Janet, so she tells us, is studying Arabic love poetry! What a fascinating subject!'

I deliberately let that remark fall into a dead silence, for I knew that Aunt Syb knew even less about Arabic love poetry than I did. Jan however was obviously not enjoying the Trethowan habit of treating an outsider as if he were not quite *there* – of talking at, around, above and below him as if he were a novice gymnast to whom they were awarding points. She said:

'What have you been doing today, Perry?'

'Going through my old home, actually,' I said. 'I've been snuffling around in the Gothic wing.'

'Ah!' said Sybilla, brightening up. 'And did you find anything? Make any Holmesian discoveries? I have wondered whether your father didn't have some *fascinating* but not entirely reputable secrets that he did not see fit to confide even to us.'

'If he did, I found out nothing about them,' I said. 'As a matter of fact, I was thinking most of the time more about my mother than my father.'

At this sudden mention of our mother, I saw Cristobel react – something between a blink and a flinch. But Sybilla ploughed on:

'Your mother! How extraordinary! You know, I'd really

forgotten all about your mother, though of course I knew you had one. You know, she was a case in point to what we've just been talking about. *Charming* woman, but not a grain of aesthetic feeling in her body. Sometimes it was difficult to remember she was there, when we were all talking!'

'She was always nice to me,' said Kate.

'I'm sure we're all nice to you, Kate dear. I don't see the point of that remark. I suppose, Peregrine, you've been sitting up there thinking that your father was a bad husband to poor Virginia, and no doubt you're right in a way, but the fact is that a little neglect was all your mother asked for, she just wanted to be left alone, so it worked out quite for the best for all parties.'

'All the Trethowans make terrible husbands,' pronounced Lawrence complacently. 'Except m'father. And he was a fool.'

It was at this point that once again the sort of noise that must have assailed Davy Crockett's ears as the Alamo fell sounded from a far corner of the house and came threateningly nearer. Daniel's eyes (which had been gazing with mildly contemptuous curiosity at the present company) now grew round with fear, and he clutched convulsively to his mother's skirts. I went and took his hand as the infant Assyrians burst in like wolves on the fold, and once more threw themselves, screaming and pummelling each other the while, into the lap of their fond grandfather.

Today it wasn't sweets they were after. They had something much more novel in their appalling little heads. As they climbed all over Lawrence's chair they screamed: 'G'anpa, we fought the policeman,' and 'G'anpa, he tried to beat me up, but I hit him back,' all crowned by the oldest boy, who let out a great crow of 'We won! We ground him in the dust!'

This din of claim and counterclaim, complaint and rodomontade, went on for some minutes, during which Peter and Maria-Luisa sauntered in, nodded to Jan (not

97

even that, actually, on Maria-Luisa's part) and helped themselves to drink. Lawrence was drooling (literally: there was dribble coming down from the side of his mouth) over his monstrous grandchildren, telling them how clever they'd been, how the idea of questioning little children was scandalous, how he'd see some questions were asked in the right quarters, and so on, until finally, by some unspoken collective decision, they swarmed off him again and went to dispute in a far corner as to who had hit the policeman the hardest. Only then did Daniel, wonderingly, come out from behind Jan's skirts and my leg.

'Not much spirit, your boy, Perry,' said Uncle Lawrence.

That got me. That really got me. 'We've tried to teach him some manners,' I said.

'Dear Perry,' cooed Sybilla. 'Such a conventional streak. I can't *think* where it comes from.'

'Probably from my mother, whom you never noticed was there,' I said.

Well, things really did seem to be starting badly: here was I working up to a right little session of snipe and countersnipe with them, whereas what I wanted was for the Harpenden Trethowans to wrangle among themselves, maul each other. I wanted to be quite out of it. One's wife so easily decides that it is you in the wrong, rather than all the rest. You may have noticed that yourselves. Fortunately, Mordred changed the subject.

'I've got you to thank for a very busy day, Perry.'

'Oh?'

'Yes. Quite a change to feel needed. Your men have been coming to me all afternoon with pictures of a vaguely Turkish character, or else with rustic scenes in horrendous greens.'

'Any luck?'

'No. I've had *Lady Mary Wortley Montagu at the Court of the Sultan*. I've had *The Death of Tamerlane*. I've had some designs Mother-dear did for *Hassan*. And some really frightful rural scenes that are simply jungles of

98

sentimentalized farm animals. But not a trace of the Hunt or the Allan.'

'At least they're doing something *useful*,' said Sybilla, 'something that will save us hiring somebody to do it. One feels that at last one is getting something back for all the imposts that the government inflicts on one.'

'It's a point of view,' I said. 'Though I'm not sure policemen make the best art detectives.'

'Those designs for *Hassan*,' pursued Sybilla meditatively. 'It was a revival that never actually came off. Your father was to do the music, Perry – lots of cymbals and wailing wind instruments. But tastes had changed, and it was too expensive. A little too blatant, too, perhaps. I wonder now if one mightn't hold a little exhibition of one's theatrical designs.'

When we had all penetrated Sybilla's use of the impersonal third person and the negative conditional tense, Lawrence said: 'You're not having an exhibition here, Syb. I've always stood out against letting in the public.'

'I didn't say *here*, Lawrence dear,' said Sybilla waspishly. 'Though, when you come to think of it, it would be appropriate. And we have to bear in mind that there is going to be a great upsurge of public interest in *us* – in us as a *family* of artists–' (especially in one of us, I thought) '–and an exhibition actually in our home would be a tremendous attraction. Quite apart from the quality of the designs themselves.'

She looked around, her head cocked like a fledgling bird waiting for a nice portion of worm. Most of us looked a bit glum, but Cristobel, who can be relied upon in the sweetness and light department, said: 'What a lovely idea, Aunt Syb! It would give you such an interest!'

Kate said: 'Shouldn't have thought we'd want *hoi polloi* all over the place.' But I thought she sounded a bit wistful. It couldn't be much of a life here for Aunt Kate, without a monster-sized ego to keep her warm.

At last it was dinner-time, and the Squealies, who had been re-enacting the snipping of the strappado cord with

yells of delight all over the available floor-space, were
bundled off back to the Elizabethan wing. We most of us
breathed sighs of relief, and as the din finally faded and died
Jan said:

'Golly, I can hear myself speak.'

Lawrence chuckled: 'Full of life, what? Aren't they little
sweeties, eh?'

But Daniel, gazing perplexedly at the door through which
they had disappeared said: 'Daddy, are those *children*?'

It was a good question. Kate and Syb and Mordred
thought it very amusing, but Lawrence muttered something
about his being a queer sort of kid, and Pete reactivated
his sneer.

'Aren't children *funny*!' said Cristobel brightly.

As we all sat down to dinner, Daniel seemed to have
regained confidence. He sat next to me on a raised chair,
and looked round at the assembled oddities as if they were
a Punch and Judy show set up especially for his benefit.
I had to keep shovelling bits of food into his mouth because
he forgot to eat, in anticipation of something happening.
He didn't have long to wait.

It was Mordred who started them off, after a covert wink
in my direction.

'Well, it will be fine for me if there *is* a big new public
interest in the family. I could probably get some publisher
or other to commission my book on you all.'

'Oh darling — money in advance!' said Syb.

'Precisely.'

'Bit parasitic all this, isn't it?' muttered Peter.

'If so, all the more necessary to suck the blood. The
good thing is that this is all coming at a time when everyone is also waking up to the real quality of Aunt Eliza's
work.'

'Dear Elizabeth,' breathed Sybilla. 'Dear sweet muddle-
headed soul. You know, I never felt the tiniest twinge of
jealousy at her success.'

'Y'fought like cat and dog when she was alive,' said
Lawrence.

A vein in Sybilla's forehead twitched. 'If we fought, we fought as *sisters*, not as fellow artists,' she said grandly. 'I'd have thought you of all people would have understood that.'

'Don't see it makes a scrap of difference, m'self,' said Kate, at her most downright tonight. 'You fought all the time anyway.'

'Being sisters is *awfully* difficult,' said Cristobel.

'Never really understood what they saw in 'Liza's stuff,' said Uncle Lawrence. 'Not that later stuff, anyway. All wispy lines and dots. Went bonkers, I'd say. Just slightly bonkers. I'll be glad to get rid of it.'

'*Rid* of it?' said Sybilla.

'Oh yes,' said Mordred, happily heaping on the coals. 'You had an offer today, didn't you, Uncle?'

'Had an enquiry. Not the only one. Had several galleries on to me these last few years. I string 'em along, keep 'em panting. The galleries mostly wanted the late stuff. They must be bonkers too. Whole world's gone slightly off-beam, what?'

'And who,' asked Sybilla coldly, 'was this enquiry *from*?'

'America. That's different. They've got the cash. Some damnfool lot of women in America somewhere. Philadelphia. They're starting a Museum of Women's Art, or some such nonsense. They've got one of Eliza's already, want some more.'

'How *fascinating*!' said Sybilla, thawing visibily as the possibilities of the idea struck her. 'I wonder if they'd like some of my designs.'

'Shouldn't wonder,' said Lawrence, raising a portion of meat painfully to his mouth. 'Was saying to Perry this morning, must be mostly rubbish they've got. No wonder they want more of 'Liza's.'

Kate had been listening greedily, while shovelling food in with hearty, open-air relish. 'I've got five of Eliza's,' she said. 'Left me in the will. I could sell one and have a holiday again. I haven't seen Bavaria for jolly ages. Dear old Berchtesgaden!'

101

'I shouldn't be *quite* sure they're yours, Kate dear,' said Sybilla, the twitch active again. 'Eliza's will, as you will remember, was a terrible mess.'

' 'Course they're mine. What do these Americans want, Lawrence?'

'All her periods. Early, middle, late. Comprehensive survey, they said. She was "one of the focal pioneers of" something or other, so they said. God, what tommyrot people talk these days!'

'Oh, goody!' said Kate, swallowing half a potato in her delight. 'I could sell them all. Eliza wouldn't mind. She always preferred her things to be seen. Apart from the portraits of us, the only things we've got here are the ones she couldn't sell.'

'Which is mostly the late stuff,' complained Lawrence. 'They got dumped here. Bits o' nonsense. I had 'em put in the rooms nobody goes in.'

'Those are the ones people want these days,' said Mordred, meditatively. 'They fetch . . .'

'And which,' interposed Sybilla, edging her troops in slowly, 'is the picture of Eliza's that they've got already?'

McWatters was serving the second helping of roast lamb, and seemed to be doing it extraordinarily slowly. Perhaps he knew the signs of approaching convulsions, and was hoping to circumvent the family's tendency to throw breakables at moments of stress (they'd all once visited the D. H. Lawrences in Italy, and watching them at it had decided it was an awfully jolly game).

Lawrence begun scrabbling in his pocket, with great difficulty, and Sybilla continued: 'Not, of course, that there's any question of *selling*. We are, after all, *custodians*—'

'Speak for yourself,' roared Lawrence. 'I'm not a custodian, I'm the bally owner.' He drew out a crumpled bit of paper, now wrapped up with one of the Squealies' sweet-papers. 'Ah yes, here it is. Where is it? Ah: they've got something they call *First Night at Covent Garden* – "wonderful confection of reds and golds and gauzy greens" the damnfool woman writes. Ever heard such rubbish?'

There was a moment of loaded silence, which I saw Mordred conducting with his left hand. Then Sybilla took off.

'She never in her life painted a picture with that title. That's *Crush Bar, Covent Garden, May 1952*. I know it! The description fits exactly!'

'Don't know why she bothered with titles,' grumbled Lawrence. 'Never looked like what they're supposed to be. I can understand abstracts, but I never got what Eliza was getting at.'

'But she was a wonderful painter,' protested Jan. 'There's a splendid late one in the Tate—'

'She was a wonderful painter, in her way,' interrupted Sybilla, and turning to Jan as if momentarily unsure who she was, 'but you're all missing the point. Whether she was good or bad is neither here nor there. She is in demand, and *Crush Bar, Covent Garden* is one of *our* paintings. One of the late ones that was here at the time of her death. When she was going through a trough, and very little was selling. The point is, they've got one of ours!'

'Y've probably got it wrong as usual, Syb,' said Lawrence.

'I have not got it wrong, Lawrence. Peter, you must remember – it used to hang in the hallway, by the Elizabethan wing—'

'Oh God, Aunt Sybilla, I can't remember every damn thing of Aunt Eliza's there is around the place. I don't take to them, quite frankly. You got it wrong about Great-Grandfather's christening spoon, so I expect you've bombed again.'

'I have not bombed! Mordred. You must remember. We moved it after her death to the south writing-room.'

'Good Lord, Mother. I was only twelve or so at the time. I don't suppose I've been in the south writing-room in the past twenty years.'

'Exactly. That's what the thief banked on. We just never go into those rooms. It's been all too easy for him! Surely *someone* remembers that picture?'

'Oddly enough, Aunt Syb, I think I do,' I said. 'It's sort of all lines and suggestions—'

'That's it. Like all the late ones. A line here, a dash of some new colour there, and the whole scene was before you.'

'You didn't think much of them at the time,' said Kate.

'As I remember it,' I said, raising my voice, 'it wasn't any sort of Impressionist thing. It's almost abstract when you first look at it, and then it begins to take shape.'

'Exactly!' said Sybilla.

'Aunt Eliza talked to me about it. She often used to talk about her paintings to me, I suppose because I was small and quiet, and hadn't much to do. She said that one was done . . . oh dear, I was so young . . . was it when Callas was singing, or something?'

'Yes! That's right! The first night of Callas's *Norma*. Lawrence, that proves it. They've got one of *our* pictures.'

'*Mine*,' said Lawrence. 'Anyway, you haven't proved anything, Syb, you old fool. You haven't even seen a photograph of the thing they've got.'

'We can soon remedy that. Perry, that policeman of yours with the Shakespearean name, he can telegraph for a photograph, can't he? This is important! The family substance is being dissipated!'

'There is no such thing as the family substance,' shouted Uncle Lawrence, getting red in the face and looking as if he would like to loosen his collar. 'There is what is mine and what is yours. You've got no sense of *meum et tuum*, you foolish creature. That damn confection in pink and gauzy whatever-it-is is mine, and I tell you now I forbid the police *or* any hysterical old women poking their over-developed noses into my affairs.'

'I'm afraid it's not quite as simple as that, Uncle Lawrence,' I put in. 'If this is connected with the murder, it may be necessary to look into it.'

'I forbid it. A man still has his rights, eh? Against officialdom's poking and prying, what?'

'I think Lawrence has popped them himself,' said Kate,

voicing the general impression, I suspect, 'and if he can, I can. I'll sell all mine.'

'The question is, which *are* yours?' said Sybilla sharply. 'You were left the pictures in your possession. You've swapped the pictures in your wing with the pictures in other wings over and over again since poor Eliza died.'

'I had to find something to go with my collection,' said Kate defensively. She turned to Jan. 'I've got an absolutely ripping collection of SS mementoes. You must come and see it. Daniel would love it. The trouble is, nothing of Eliza's really *went*. Finally I decided on *Coventry Razed, 1940*. I know I own that because Eliza gave it to me.'

'Kate! She did not! That was a personal gift to me!'

'Oh rot, Syb. She never gave you anything. You were always so sniffy about her work. The only reason you had several when she died was because you went and grabbed things from the house while she lay dying.'

'Catherine! Such lies!'

'You knew what was in the will. The only thing you had of your own was a little abstract called *Shifting Planes* which you'd bought to spite her because you knew she was no good at abstracts.'

'She's deranged,' announced Sybilla.

'No, I'm not. I'm the only one who really knows what's been going on in this house. Leo had hardly any paintings either, because he didn't like any member of the family being more talented than he was. He grabbed more when she died, too. I saw him smuggling them up to the Gothic wing.'

'They'll all have to be given back,' said Lawrence with a malignant relish. 'They're all mine.'

'I know *Festival Scene* is ours,' said Cristobel, with a trace of family spirit, not to mention family acquisitiveness. 'Mine, I should say. Because Daddy told me that Aunt Eliza gave it to him.'

'Hardly evidence,' said Lawrence. 'It'll all have to be given back. And that Dali you've got.'

'I certainly won't give it back. Daddy bought it, with his own money. He told me so.'

'Nonsense. It was bought by Eliza when he was still in short trousers. If it's not back tomorrow I'll go and see m'lawyers!'

I foresaw an eternity of litigation, a Jarndyce and Jarndyce case that would outlive us, the fourth generation of Trethowans. Sybilla seemed to sense the danger too, for she began to draw in her horns.

'This is all too silly,' she said. 'If there is one place for Eliza's paintings it is here. Nothing will be sold. Of course.'

'Suddenly become head of the family, have you, Syb?' enquired Uncle Lawrence. 'That's something no woman will ever be, thanks to Grandfather Josiah. Sensible chap. Well, as far as I'm concerned there's no reason why Eliza's daubs should be here. She didn't even like the place.'

'Lawrence! What nonsense! She loved Northumberland!'

'She hated Harpenden. She said it was a festering sore on the body of the country. She said it got bigger and uglier every time she came back. Hardly ever did come back till the end. Lived in London. Well, London can have her.'

'She never lived in Philadelphia.'

'Well, I don't want her around me here. It's like living in the Turner rooms of the Tate. We're not a damned Museum. I prefer those Victorian things she used to sneer at. At least they're lively, what?'

I began to think that on the whole I preferred Uncle Lawrence senile: he could be a right Josiah Trethowan if he really set his mind to it. Without the strength that comes from a truly bullish stupidity, of course.

'Well, of course we all love the Victorian pictures now,' said Sybilla. 'We've come round to them, as no doubt Eliza would have, too. They're part of the house, too; part of the Trethowan heritage. It's simply not up to you suddenly to make a decision to get rid of parts of it. You're robbing us of our common patrimony.'

'It's not common! It's mine!'

'When, after all, you're not going to live forever—'

'I'll outlive you! I'll outfox you, too, if you try anything!
I've still got my wits about me!'

'On occasion,' said Sybilla.

'The main thing is, it's mine. The house is mine – you're
all here on sufferance, remember that. Don't even pay me
a penny rent. The grounds are mine, the pictures are mine,
the furniture is mine, the money is mine. None of you can
alter that. And it will all go to little Pietro—'

'Via me,' said Pete.

'Via you. *If* you outlive me. Talk about custody of the
family heritage! I'm the custodian! And I'm not answerable
to *any* of you. D'ye hear me, Syb? I've been too soft! I'm
the head of the family! One word from any of you, and out
you all go!'

I saw Aunt Syb's hand reaching towards a side plate, and
I pushed back my chair and made moves to go. Much more
of this and Uncle Lawrence would have another spectacular
stroke and the third generation Trethowans would have
suffered further decimation in the course of a couple of days.
It was all quite deplorable. Daniel had been so fascinated
he had forgotten to eat his caramel custard, absolutely his
favourite sweet. You can't blame him: as an exercise in
geriatric awfulness I remember nothing like it since
Whatever Happened To Baby Jane? or the last years of
President de Gaulle. As we all broke up in disorder I
muttered our excuses to Uncle Lawrence, and said we had
to get Daniel back to the Marquis of Danby and off to bed.
Lawrence didn't seem to hear. He was puckering his old
lips in triumph and looking round as if he'd won a famous
victory. I dashed off to Tim to acquire a car, and while I
was about it, I tipped the wink about Philadelphia, and
suggested he get a photo by the fastest possible method.
He tried to show me details of my father's financial affairs,
and his will, but I said I had to get out of this madhouse,
and made my escape.

The funny thing is that by the time I got back to the main
block, they were all having coffee in the drawing-room, and
palsy-walsy as could be. Sybilla was telling Jan some funny

story from Aunt Eliza's death-bed. Morrie grinned at me conspiratorially, and I had to be friendly back. He had done a marvellous job, and quite unobtrusively. I suppose if you live with them you know every sensitive spot, and can effortlessly put your finger on it in a way that sets them howling. Maria-Luisa saw the exchange of glances between us, and lowered.

Anyway, driving back to the village I was quite irrationally proud of the evening's performance, especially since it was put on without benefit of rehearsal. It was Daniel who had enjoyed it most: no sooner were we out of the house than he started jumping up and down with delight at the spectacle he had just witnessed.

'Daddy, Daddy — they behaved very badly, didn't they, Daddy?'

I thought this was no time to beat about the bush with specious excuses.

'Yes, they did, Dan.'

'Can we go and watch them do it again tomorrow?'

'No.'

'Poor old dears,' said Jan, 'they—'

'Cut that out, Jan. Don't give me the "poor old dears" line. They've been like this as long as I can remember. They're a thoroughly repulsive collection of crazed egotists, and always have been.'

'Well, at least they're individuals,' she retorted.

'Oh my God, individuals. If there ever was a ghastly warning against cultivating your ego, aiming at total self-fulfilment, doing your own thing regardless — the Trethowan family is it. If they'd given them their own television show twenty years ago, the 'sixties would never have happened.'

'Well, it's better than my parents. Stuck in front of the telly the whole time, and if you drop round to see them they complain they missed one of Annie Walker's lines because they had to open the door.'

'Your parents scarcely exist. There must be something between being like them and being like the Trethowans.'

'Aren't we going to see them again?' asked Daniel, downcast.

'No,' I said.

'Yes, darling,' said Jan. 'I told Aunt Sybilla I'd go and see the gardens tomorrow.'

'Oh, God!' I said. 'Well, keep in the open where you can be seen. I don't trust any of that lot an inch. I'd put your old jeans on. She'll get you doing the weeding. The grounds are obviously too much for two men. Just to look at it has me itching to get at a spade.'

'You see? You're feeling at home there already. I can just see the way you've been settling in.'

Well, we started a good old slanging match over that, but as a matter of fact we had a very nice rest-of-evening: we played with Daniel and I heard all his news; we put him to bed and went and had a pint in the bar, where the landlady deferred to me in a way that tickled Jan pink; and then – well, there isn't any more of the day's doings that you need to know of for this story.

Except that in the middle of the night I woke up, and sensed that Jan was awake too. And as I put my arm around her, she said:

'Perry, are you awake? There's something I've been meaning to say to you all evening since we got away.'

'What's that, love?'

'You do realize that Cristobel is pregnant, don't you?'

CHAPTER 11

BROTHER AND SISTER

Breakfast was served next morning in a poky little dining-
room in the new extension to the Marquis. (I disapproved
of the extension, of course, as all returned travellers
disapprove of things that have happened since their time,
however much they disliked what was there before.) Mrs
Killigrew, the new landlady, waited on us with a quite
killing deference, which she no doubt thought was our due
as part of the family at the Big House. Coming from
Birmingham, she was living in the past, I suppose. Jan, I
am ashamed to say, lapped it up.

'Any moment now she'll be calling you the Young
Master,' she whispered.

'Is Daddy the Young Master?' demanded Daniel.

'No, dear. He's not.'

'Who is, then?'

We thought. 'Well, Peter, I suppose,' I said, and Jan and
I collapsed choking with laughter over our poached eggs.
Mrs Killigrew, returning, seemed to be noting down that
seemly grief in times of mourning was no longer *de rigueur*
in the best families.

'Are you sure?' I asked Jan, when she had gone out.
'About what you said last night?'

'Of course I'm sure.' She put on her wise-family-friend
look. 'A woman always knows.'

'What does a woman always know?' asked Daniel.

'Everything, darling. Are you going to have a big-
brotherly thing with her, Perry? Demand she go into

110

seclusion at Ostend and conceal the family shame?'

'Oh, don't be crass, Jan. Of course, I feel a bit responsible for her, but she's all of thirty, and in fact I think it would be a really good thing for her, if not for the kid, and I'd be quite pleased, only—'

'Only?'

'Well, I'd be quite pleased if I thought it was one of the gardeners, or the vicar, or somebody.'

'She sings in the choir. Perhaps it is the vicar. They're awfully liberated these days.'

'Only the homosexuals. The rest keep it all in, same as ever. But I know who it is. I've been remembering our first chat, and it was "poor Morrie's got so much to do" and "Daddy kept picking on poor Morrie" and all that kind of thing. I know what's been happening. He's been working on her pity. The neglected spaniel approach.'

'Mordred? Are you sure? Anyway, she may like him.'

'Hmm. But she would keep it in the family, wouldn't she? All those healthy, normal people out there in the big world, and she goes bedding down with Cousin Morrie. It would be so much better if she got right away from Harpenden. But I bet she won't. Not just when she's come in to what she's been waiting for.'

'She doesn't inherit the wing, does she?'

'Sounds like shares in a chicken. No, of course she doesn't. You heard Uncle Lawrence doing his "Mine – all Mine!" stuff last night. But she'll stay on – she's part of the family circus by now, even if she doesn't do much more than show people to their seats. Besides, she obviously has a strong sense of her rights. It'll take her longer than a pregnancy to establish her claim on what's in the wing. I wouldn't give much for her chances of keeping the Dali, I'm afraid.'

'You're assuming that Mordred won't marry her?'

'I suppose they'd have gone and done it already if they were going to. What would they marry on?'

'There's Morrie's book.'

'I don't know much about publishing, but I should guess

111

that anyone who married in the expectation of royalties these days would really take a prize in the foolish virgin stakes.'

'Is our family royalties, Daddy?' asked Daniel, and brought this conversation to an end.

After breakfast Jan said she'd wander round the village and see if she could pick up any gossip. I gave my blessing to this project with an inward chuckle. The village of Harpenden had done nothing but gossip about the Trethowans for the last ninety-five years, ever since the first workmen had arrived to dig foundations that would have been more appropriate for a Crusader castle. The villagers had got more hand-outs and free drinks out of British newspapermen than anybody in the world, except perhaps the islanders of Mustique. That should keep Jan happy for the morning.

When I got myself to the Gothic wing I was met by an interesting sight. Tim Hamnet and Constable Smith were having a right old one-twoer with two men whom I took to be the gardeners. They had been caught trying to remove the Dali from my father's study. They were under orders, apparently, to take it to the main block. Uncle Lawrence, it seemed, was having another of his good days today, and was acting firmly on the principles enunciated so brutally last night. However, in this case, as least, he was frustrated: nothing was to be touched in the murder wing (as — if he'd had a grain of sense left — the silly old bugger should have realized for himself). In the end the gardeners saw they were on to a bad wicket and sloped off. No doubt they had several calls of a similar nature to make in the other wings.

Anyway, Tim and I went up to the library, as being more comfortable than the big room on the ground floor which I was increasingly coming to think of as the Torture Chamber, and we sat around and had a good old natter about the case. I won't go into it in detail, because I've given you most of the stuff already, one way and another, and I want to get this story over within a reasonable time, but there were a couple of interesting things emerged from Tim's side of the conversation. The first of these was the will. No great surprises there. I half suspected I was going to be left some derisory object to underline his contempt for me: a pair of old socks, or his musical manuscripts or something. But no. I was not so much as mentioned. I was pleased: it seemed to keep our mutual antipathy pure and abstract, as it had been since the day I left. Everything went to 'my daughter Cristobel' (he didn't even bother with a 'dear'): money, investments, possessions – many of the last being specified, including the Dali. In fact, I had a feeling that one look at that list would have given Uncle Lawrence apoplexy. The scientific apparatus in the Torture Chamber was not mentioned. Presumably it went to Cristobel. Suitably adapted, it might form the basis of a good little gymnasium for her.

The other thing of interest was the money. My father's financial state. Here I admit my earlier guesses were proved wrong. I was surprised – and no end pleased, for Cristobel's sake – to learn that he was worth all of thirty thousand pounds, quite apart from shares, pictures, furniture, and rare editions of nasty books. Not at all bad, for my papa.

'Anything shady about it?' I asked Tim.

'Hmm, well, I'm not entirely happy, let's put it that way. I'll tell you why. You see, I've got his bank accounts for the last ten years or so. Now, on the face of it, it's a perfectly dull little record, with nothing in the least suspicious there—'

'I saw his last book of stubs upstairs,' I said.

'Precisely. Booksellers, this Percival character—'

'The wondrous artificer.'

'—whatever you like to call him. And cheques to your sister for the housekeeping. Pretty generous ones, too, so they obviously included pocket-money-cum-wage for herself. Nothing wrong with that. Now, the trouble is, they keep being interrupted for long periods. No housekeeping cheques. Then they start up again. Then there's another long break.'

'I see. Meaning, you think, that my papa somehow or other came by largish sums of cash, which he stashed away

113

(it being difficult to account for them otherwise) and used for the housekeeping and personal expenses for a bit, till they ran out. Later on he got access to more. Is that how you see it?'

'Pretty much like that.'

'Meaning, conceivably, pictures – is that what you think? What does Chris say to that?'

'That's the trouble. She denies it absolutely. She stands me out that she was paid every week by cheque for the housekeeping expenses. Perhaps once or twice in cash, she concedes, but otherwise always by cheque. I keep telling her this can't be so, she keeps telling me it is. I don't like to say this, but she's not too bright, your sister, Perry.'

'She's all right,' I said defensively. 'She's got more sense than most of this lot.'

'That's another of your faint compliments, I suppose. Well, if you talk to her again, would you try to convince her that if she'd been paid by cheque regularly, I'd have a record of it?'

'Oh, I'll be talking to her,' I said. 'I'll try. But you know my family by now. As the lady says in Thurber: "Mere proof won't convince me." '

Chris was apparently up and about, as she called it, and I finally came upon her on the far side of the lake, sitting in a little ornamental summerhouse that no doubt seemed to Great-Grandfather Josiah to add a Marie-Antoinette touch to his grounds, but now merely augmented the general sense of neglect and decay. Chris was deep in thought, but now and then she leant out and pulled at the branches and creeping tentacles of shrubs that threatened to take over the summerhouse.

'Chris,' I said.

'Oh, hello, Perry.'

'Why didn't you tell me, Chris?'

'Tell you?' The words jumped out of her mouth, and she tensed up in a terribly defensive posture.

'That you were pregnant.'

'Oh, that . . . I didn't want to worry you, on top of all this. It'll have to come out soon. But not yet. Wait till all this has . . . died down. Did Janet notice?'

'Yes. I suppose Sybilla has, too.'

'Oh, no, I don't think so. She never notices people.'

'You don't think you ought to tell her?'

'Oh, no, Perry! I couldn't! If I told anybody, it would be Kate.'

'Yes, I suppose she might be better. You really ought to get away from Harpenden, Chris. You've got money of your own now. You could manage it, and it would be much less . . . unpleasant.'

'Oh, no, I wouldn't want that, Perry! Harpenden's my home. It's where . . . everyone is. They'll all understand when they get used to the idea. We're a very unconventional family.'

'Hmmm. So the theory goes. The point is, it's the most unrestful place in the world to have a baby in, particularly in these circumstances. Oh, why did you have to keep it in the family, Chris?'

'The family's all I've got,' she said. 'You hate them. I wouldn't expect you to understand.'

'It's nothing to do with whether I hate them or not. In any case, I don't hate Mordred. But it doesn't seem right for the kid, growing up in a house full of elderly maniacs, with his father around, doing nothing, and not married to his mother . . .'

Chris had shot me a glance, but her mouth still was pursed into an obstinate line. 'Family patterns are changing these days,' she said, as if it were something she'd learned by rote. Suddenly her voice broke: 'Oh, Perry, you don't think it will matter, about being cousins, do you? I've been so worried about that . . .'

'No, no, Chris. It's an old superstition,' I said (without having much idea whether it was or not, but Chris is so helpless and pathetic at times that she makes you want to soothe her down at any price).

'Then I don't see why things shouldn't turn out all right,'

said Chris, setting her chin high in the air. 'And you never know . . .'

Marriage, I thought. One could be quite sure that what Chris would really want, in these circumstances, was marriage. Well, I'd better keep off that subject till I'd investigated the ground a bit further. For all I knew it could eventually be possible. Golly, I thought, I bet Aunt Syb's been stashing it away over the years. To change the subject, I said: 'Chris, why did you lie to the Inspector?'

'I did not, Perry!' All her defensiveness came back, and she reacted with irrational pugnaciousness.

'Look, love, you can't have been paid the housekeeping money each week by cheque, otherwise we'd have a record of the cheques in his account. There are long gaps, Chris.'

'He must have had more than one account.'

'In that case, there should have been more than one kind of cheque that he paid you with. Were there?'

'Yes . . . Yes, I think there were.'

'What was the other bank's name?'

'I . . . I can't remember, Perry.'

'Chris, what on earth is this? What are you trying to do? There's no reason on earth why he should not have paid you in cash. Why are you denying it?'

'Because he didn't! He paid me by cheque, every week. You've got a cheek, Perry, coming and questioning me like this, and saying I've been lying. I'm the one who looked after him. I'm the one who knows. You resent my getting his money!'

That was so irrational it floored me. 'I do not resent it, Chris. It's what I've always wanted for you. We just stopped the outside men lifting off your Dali, by the way.'

'The Dali!'

'You're going to have to fight to keep that, I'm afraid. But you should have a better chance with the Aunt Elizas. The trouble is, if you're going to fight Lawrence, you'll have to stay here. I still think it would be better to get out. In fact, I think you'd have done better to get out long ago.'

116

'How could I? Who would have looked after him? It was my job. Mummy said so.'

'Mother? When did she say that?'

Chris, for some reason, looked as if she could have bitten out her tongue.

'In . . . before she died. Before she died she said it was up to me look after Daddy after she'd gone. Oh, go *away*, Perry. You said you'd save me from all those questions, and now you're doing it yourself. I'm not well, you know. I shouldn't . . .'

'OK, OK, Chris. I'm going now. Look, just one more thing: remember , if there's any trouble here, Jan and I are always there to help.'

She looked rebellious. Then, to get rid of me, she said: 'All right. I know you mean well, Perry.'

But you blunder in in your copper's boots where angels ought to fear to tread, seemed to be the general implication. I got up and wandered away round the lake and back to the house, deep in thought. What was it eating Chris? One thing I was pretty sure of: our poor mother had not commended Father to Chris's care just before she died. For a start, Chris was only eight at the time. And secondly, we were about as close as it was possible to be, Chris and I, just before Mother's death and in the years immediately after. Naturally. And she would have told me of a thing like that, because it's the sort of trust Chris would take very seriously, and get a big conscientious thing about.

And yet I didn't get the idea she was lying. In fact, it had come out seemingly involuntarily, regretted immediately. And though it might seem a pretty repulsive thing to do, calling on a girl like Chris to devote her life to looking after a nasty old crackpot like our father, nevertheless, the idea was perfectly typical of my mother: she was still emotionally in the world of 1750 or thereabouts, and the pious hope that Chris would devote herself to her father's well-being would have seemed entirely natural, indeed only right, to her. I asked myself how the wish had been communicated. And I came up with the answer: by letter.

117

I walked round and round the garden, thinking about this and other things: the pictures, the *mise-en-scène* of the murder, the scissors in the plant-pot. I spoke to the gardeners, who had finished their deeds of retrieval around the house, and were busy rehearsing the story of Aunt Sybilla's pink fits for later retelling in the Marquis. I recognized one of them as being the most junior of the outdoor staff in my young days. We talked about the grounds, and what needed to be done, and how you couldn't get the labour, in spite of all this unemployment, and how you couldn't expect two men to do the work of eight, and so on. I began to feel like a member of the gentry, being matey with the peasantry. I was glad Jan wasn't there to overhear. Finally I landed up round the front of the house and was hailed from the Gothic wing by Tim Hamnet.

' 'Morning, Perry. Back on duty, I hope? By the way, no luck with Philadelphia. The Museum's closed until Monday, and no power on earth's going to get them to open up and let the police photograph the thing. That's the message; I suspect the cops themselves aren't putting their backs into it.'

'Damn their hides. I suppose with their murder rate the odd country-house killing seems an epicurean luxury. By the by, I had an idea about those pictures − bit of a long shot, but−'

'Give.'

'Well, if you'd got pictures like those to dispose of, who do you think would be interested?'

Hamnet was a bit at sea. 'National Gallery?'

'Wrong. They've got nothing British later than Turner.'

'That other one − the Tate.'

'Right. But if there was anything shady about the deal, you'd be a bit wary at approaching anywhere so well known. Their purchases tend to be well publicized. Then there're several provincial galleries with a strong line in Victorian stuff − Birmingham, for example − and of course we ought to approach them. But on the whole the same applies. What would be better would be to approach somewhere a bit less

. . . how shall I say? . . . exposed. See what I mean? Somewhere not quite so well known.'

'I get you. Could a small place afford them?'

'They could afford the Allan. He has no particular market value. And it occurs to me that the place that would be most likely to be interested in *Lord Byron Reposing in the House of a Turkish Fisherman After Having Swum the Hellespont* would be—'

'Yes?'

'Newstead Abbey. Byron's home.'

'Where's that?'

'Not far from Nottingham. Do you think it would be worthwhile giving them a tinkle?'

'Surely. We don't lose anything by it. I'd do it myself, but I'm waiting to interview little Mordred. Anyway, you know your stuff on that sort of thing. You'd do it better.'

So I trolled off quite happily and entered the house. Then I was presented with a poser. Where did I phone from? I had intended using the phone in the Main Hall, but if there was an extension in the kitchens, as I suspected, that was about the last thing I ought to do. I ruled out Sybilla as too agog, and Peter as all too conceivably implicated, and I landed up with Aunt Kate. So I made for the Georgian wing, and of course found her thoroughly delighted to be of help.

'Ring from here? 'Course you can, Perry! Tickled pink, really. Don't trust the others, I suppose. Is it top secret? Anyway, come on in.'

I went in, averting my eyes from the signed photograph of the late German Führer, given a place of honour in the cluttered little hallway.

'It's not exactly top secret, but I would like it to be private. It's not just an extension you've got here, is it?'

'Not on your life. We each have our own phone, pay our own bills. Old stingyboots Lawrence sees to that. You can have the study phone if you like. Come on, we'll take the lift. Upsadaisy!'

I'd forgotten the lift. Lifts had been installed in the

Georgian wing after the car accident in 1939 which killed my grandmother and left my grandfather an invalid for the rest of his life. Kate was the only child at home, and she had taken care of him, at least until her internment, in this wing that had later become her own (or rather her own, subject to the whim of Lawrence, or – rather more dangerously – Peter, in the not too distant future). We got out at the third floor, and she popped me in through the study door.

'There it is,' she said cheerfully. 'You can have a look at my collection while you're talking. Be worth a lot When The Time Comes. I'll be downstairs. Toodle-oo.'

No wonder she made a quick escape. Her 'study' in fact housed her proud collection of Nazi mementoes. As I got on to Directory Enquiries my eye rested on medals from the desert campaign, Iron Crosses, and pictures of the heroic action against the Polish ghetto. I closed my eyes. Really, I had to try to think of Aunt Kate not as she was now, an overgrown product of St Trinian's, but as she had been for much of her adult life, a besotted admirer of a regime that even the most morally undeveloped could perceive as evil. Could that old Kate have been totally obliterated by the 'breakdown' of last year?

I got the number of Newstead quite easily, but after that things did not go quite so well. I was answered by a helpful but rather hesitant male voice, which was obviously not at all pleased when I said I wanted to ask a question about the house.

'Look, could you ring back Monday? There'll be someone around then. I'm just a student, sitting in, you know, and none of the regulars will be back till next week.'

'It's quite a simple question, about a picture. It's a big one, I'd guess, so you ought to be able to locate it.'

'Yes, well, you see I'm a student of psychology. My mum knows one of the gardeners. The fact is, most of the visitors here know more than I do.'

I sighed. I knew that sort of literary shrine. 'Look, my name is Trethowan. I'm a policeman and it's an urgent matter.'

'I say, are you *the* Trethowan? Whose dad got done in when he was getting himself a bit sado-masochistic fun? That case is just killing me. I've just been reading all about you in the *Excess*.'

'Oh, God,' I said.

'They call you Big Perry. Your aunt told the *Excess* you gave her the most wonderful feeling of safety.'

'My aunt gives me the most wonderful feeling of a pain in the arse,' I said.

'Would you like a snap diagnosis of your father's mental condition?' asked Little Brightness at the other end.

'I understood my father's mental condition without benefit of psychiatry before I was into my teens,' I said. 'Look, about this picture—'

'OK. But I don't see what pictures have to do with it.'

'Yours not to reason why. Read next Monday's *Excess* and you might find out. It's a picture called *Lord Byron Reposing in the House of a Turkish Fisherman After Having Swum the Hellespont*. It must be fairly easy to identify.'

'Hell, it's not even easy to say! How am I supposed to identify it?'

'Well, he can't have much on, I would imagine. And there must be a sort of Turkish element in the picture.'

'I suppose you're right. Hey, wait: there is a picture like that. Sort of sexy, in an ethereal Victorian kind of a way. Where is it, now?'

'Could you trot round and have a look for it?'

'Sure thing. Hold on.'

I hung on, and cast my eyes around my aunt's loathsome souvenirs. The Turks and the Nazis – both rapists of Greece. There was a picture of tanks entering Athens. Before long my budding Freud came back on the line.

'Yes. I've found it. It's like what you said. Lots of white flesh. Hey, you'd have thought he'd have had a tan, wouldn't you?'

'Gentlemen didn't tan in those days. White was sexy.'

'Is that for real? I thought sexy was always sexy.'

'You can't have seen any silent films. Keep to the subject.

121

Is there anything about the picture in the catalogue?'

'Catalogue? . . . Oh yeah, wait a tick . . . Yes, here it is: *Lord Byron* etc by William Allan. Painted, 1831. Acquired for Newstead in 1979.'

'It doesn't say who from?'

'Nope.'

'Any idea who would know?'

'Not a clue. Why don't you ring Monday, eh?'

'Look, is there a list in the catalogue of the Trustees, and the committee, and such like, for Newstead Abbey?'

'Haven't a notion. Where would it be?'

'Try the first page.'

'Oh yeah. Here they are. Local bigwigs and some pro-fessors.'

'Could you dictate their names to me?'

And so, finally, I got them, and the other end rang off, very cheery, saying if I wanted more help, just to ring back. I decided that the checking of the list of trustees to see if they could help over the buying of the Allan could be done by Tim or one of his team. The main thing was, I'd established that one of the pictures missing from Harpenden had indeed recently been sold (I was damn sure it hadn't been given to Newstead!). Now we had to decide where to go from there.

I went down the stairs. I'm never entirely happy in rickety old lifts: they sometimes give the impression that my weight is something in the nature of a last straw. When I got down to the hall, Kate was waiting, like a well-set-up vulture.

'Get what you wanted?'

'Yes, Aunt Kate, I think so.'

'I say, Perry?'

'Yes?'

'You haven't inquisited me yet.'

'I haven't inquisited anyone, Aunt Kate.'

'Oh, you fibber. You've talked to people. You've talked to Mordred and Peter, I know. The other one inquisited me, but I didn't tell him much. There are things one doesn't talk about outside the family.'

122

'Well, we could have a little chat, Aunt Kate,' I said, thinking she wasn't so entirely round the bend that she couldn't be useful.

'Oh, spiffing! When?'

'Well, I've just got to deliver this list to the Superintendent. I could be back in twenty minutes or so.'

'Oh, goody,' said Kate. 'Then you can stay to lunch!'

CHAPTER 12

LOW CUISINE

Of course, I had to admit to myself that I'd asked for it. Walked straight into it with my chin out. One look at the clock, then showing after twelve, should have warned me of the danger. Even then I could have said I'd come back at half past four, and she could have given me afternoon tea and we would have both been happy. You can't do much with afternoon tea. But I was caught off balance, and all I could do was to produce a ghastly grin of acquiescence.

I went and shared my bit of news about *Lord Byron* with Tim Hamnet, and he set one of his men on to ringing round the various Trustees of Newstead to see if any of them had been involved in the buying of the picture. I also procured one of those little plastic bags that policemen use for sending specimens along to the forensic labs. I felt an awful coward. It was obvious that eating with Aunt Kate was an essential part of the Trethowan experience. One ought to face up to it, as to one's first beating at public school, one's first taste of fire in battle. It wasn't as if I had a particularly delicate stomach: after all, I'd been eating in army and police canteens for most of my adult life. One develops a certain toughness of the gut.

Still, I have to admit that as I strode resolutely back towards the Georgian wing, I was in a moderately filthy mood. And it wasn't improved by my coming upon Mordred in the main hall: quite apart from the business with Chris, I was irritated by the mere look of him: he had no business

124

to go around with that air of oh-so-appetizing agelessness, like an academic Cliff Richard.

He said: 'Hello, Perry. Bloodhounds still hot on the scent, are they?'

I just snapped: 'I want to talk to you later.'

He looked hurt and injured, like a favourite courtier spurned by the Sun King.

I steamed ahead, the battleship *Resolute* preparing for an engagement, and rang the doorbell to the Georgian wing. Kate was all over me, of course, and beside herself with the unaccustomed pleasure of being hostess. She was wearing one of her inevitable suits (I remember her confiding to me that as fashions changed she took the hems up two inches, or let them down two inches), and over it a magnificent flowered apron. She looked the very embodiment of *Kirche, Küche, Kinder*. She marched me into the sitting-room – normally decorated, thank God, without tributes to the heroes of the Third Reich, though I noticed gaps on the walls, caused, no doubt, by Lawrence's depredations – and she sat me down in a capacious, comfortable armchair. All the time she fussed over me in her gruff way, like an Old English Sheepdog penning up a prize ram.

'Won't be a sec,' she bellowed, darting off to the kitchen. 'It's nearly ready. I love risotto, don't you? You can put absolutely everything in!'

Well, I suppose that is the theory. I had an awful feeling that even the most exuberant of Italian housewives would still exercise a modicum of discretion that was beyond my Aunt Kate. I sat there, helpless, a lamb to the gastronomic slaughter.

Kate poked her head round the door.

'Dandelion or parsnip?'

'I beg your—'

'Wine, you chump! I've got the parsnip chilled.'

'Oh,' I said, being fiendishly cunning. 'The parsnip, then.'

She bore in the wine, in superb nineteenth-century goblets. She bore in a great tureen and served out the risotto with a liberal hand, ignoring my gestures to stop.

I received my plate, and tried not to look too closely. The rice was soggy with overcooking, but it was in any case a minor component. The major part consisted, if my eyes did not deceive me, of scraps of beef, bits of turnip and beetroot, hacked up sardines and diced tinned peaches. And some squares of what could very easily be dog food. I shut my eyes and thought of England.

'Lawrence sent the gardeners today,' announced Aunt Kate. She had seized a fork in her large paw and now began shovelling in with gusto, as once she must have gobbled camp food in the Bavarian mountains, while Czechoslovakia bled. 'After my pictures.'

'Did they take any?'

'Took two. When they came back for more, I'd got my Mauser out of the Collection. Scared 'em silly, and they took to their heels. Wasn't loaded, but they weren't game to risk it. World's gone soft!'

'Uncle Lawrence certainly seems to be concerned about his property.'

'Got a fit of the meanies,' said Aunt Kate complacently. 'Happens when you get old.'

'I suppose so,' I said. 'I never remember him being miserly when I was young.'

Aunt Kate shook her head vigorously. 'Wasn't. Didn't care about money. Above it. Paid out oodles to that second wife of his. Pete's mother. What do they call it? Alimony.'

'Why did he do that?'

'Keep her quiet. He was having an affair with a Marchioness or somebody. Paid out so she wouldn't be named as co-respondent, so he said.'

'Doesn't sound like a Trethowan. I'd have expected him to revel in the publicity.'

'Yes, you would, wouldn't you? We are a bit blatant, aren't we, Perry?'

'The tiniest bit, now and then.'

'Anyway, he didn't have to shell out for long, because she died.'

'Had he paid alimony to his first wife too?'

'Oh, no. They were never divorced. She was a Catholic. She died before the war some time.'

'Didn't have much luck with his wives, Uncle Lawrence.'

'They didn't have much luck with *him*,' said Aunt Kate emphatically. 'Always sniffing round someone or other. Wouldn't think it, to look at him now!'

'How bad is Uncle Lawrence? In health, I mean.'

'Has his off days, as you saw. He'd had three days like that when you saw him. Sleeps here with me, these days. Think he puts it on a bit, sometimes. Like a child. Wants attention. Likes to be fussed. Knows more about what's going on than he lets on to. Still, I play along with him. Not like Syb and Leo—'

'Oh?'

'They're crazy, the way they provoke him. Provoked, in one case. Ought to think of the future. He'll pop off if he has another of those strokes. Then where will we be? Awful swine, that Peter. Wouldn't think twice about throwing us all out into the snow. You enjoying this? It's scrumptious, isn't it?'

I was masticating thoughtfully a forkful that seemed to include a bony bit of kipper and a lump of marshmallow. I washed it down with a great gulp of parsnip wine and said: 'This wine's awfully good.'

'I'll fill you up,' said Aunt Kate, and trotted off to the kitchen, while I transferred a judicious amount of the nauseating goo to my little forensic bag, and stuffed it into my trouser pocket.

'What did you mean,' I asked, as she settled herself down again and resumed her enthusiastic fork-lift job on her plateful, 'about Father provoking Uncle Lawrence? Did they have any big rows?'

'Not out in the open. Too cunning for that. Of course, your father sniped. He couldn't help that, you know, Perry. He was a sniper by nature. But they kept the row under cover.'

'What makes you think they had one?'

127

'Because,' said Aunt Kate triumphantly, 'he took him walking!'

'What?'

'They went walking together – a long tour round the grounds. Well, Leo walking, Lawrence being wheeled. Can you imagine your father wheeling that chair? He *never* did it. Not his style at all. But he had to do it, because it was the only way they could be alone. So they could row.'

It made sense. 'Did it happen often?'

'Just once since the stroke. About ten days ago. I'd've trailed them if I'd known. I used to be a marvellous tracker! Put on weight a bit since, but I bet the twigs wouldn't crack under me!'

'You've no idea what it could be about?'

'Not a notion. Chrissy, perhaps?' She looked at me in a sideways way to see if I knew, and was disappointed when she saw I did.

'I see you've noticed, Aunt Kate.'

' 'Course I've noticed. Got eyes. Saw it start. Saw what they were up to. Glances across the table. Footsy. Trotting off to the summerhouse.'

'Did you discuss it with anyone?'

' 'Course I didn't. Kept it to m'self. Silly gel, though. Got no pride.'

'It's going to be difficult for her, though, Aunt Kate. She may need a bit of support.'

'I'll support her. Can't blame a girl for going off the rails once in a while. Drive you a bit potty, looking after a little squirt like Leo all day long. I know. I did it for my father. And he was *nice*.'

'Cristobel says it was our mother who charged her to look after Father. I don't see how it could be . . .'

' 'Course it was. Cristobel got this letter thing.'

'Ah! She did, then.'

'That's right. You know, sent by the lawyers, marked "to be opened when she is twenty-one" or something like that. Bit soppy of Virginia, I thought. Old-fashioned. But then she was. Anyway, your mother — God rest her soul, because she was a *good* woman, Perry, I don't mean to speak against her — said she should regard her father as a sacred charge. I couldn't see Leo as the Ark of the Covenant m'self, but you know Chrissy. Went around for days after she got it, telling everybody about it.'

'Was there anything else in it?'

'Lot of guff. Embarrassing. About a mother's love. You know. People shouldn't write stuff like that. When you're gone, you're gone. Nobody gives a damn what you say. Look at Franco!'

'It's odd she should write a letter like that to Cristobel, but not one to me.'

'Post Office's gone all to pot these days,' said Kate, who seemed a bit distracted. 'I say, more wine?'

Blessedly she bore my glass to the kitchen, and I had recourse again to my bag, at the same time managing to extract from my mouth something that seemed to be nutty fudge. Look, I won't tell you anything more about that damned risotto. I don't want to be accused of writing gastronomic pornography.

I wasn't willing to let the subject of the letter drop, so when Kate came back waving another bumper of parsnip wine (the only good thing about which was that it did not taste of parsnip), I said: 'I wonder if my mother did send me a letter. And I wonder what happened to it.'

''Spect Leo destroyed it,' said Kate cheerfully. 'Lawyers probably sent it here. I can just see him. Probably read it over, smiled his nasty little smile, tore it up and put it in the fire. Bet that's what he did.'

Yes, I could see him too. Except for that little note in his drawer. I said: 'But if he were to hide it . . .'

'Plenty of room to hide it,' said Kate, in the understatement of the year. 'But I think he'd destroy it, unless it contained something important. He hated you, you know, Perry!'

'Yes, I think he did,' I agreed. 'I wondered at one point whether Cristobel wasn't exaggerating, but I think

129

it must have been true. All because I called him a mediocrity!'

'That's the one thing none of them will admit!' said Kate. 'Got to be plumped up the whole time. Like cushions. Calling him a mediocrity was worse than hitting him. He hated you, I tell you. He certainly wouldn't have put a postage stamp on a letter from your mother to you.'

'Yes, I see that. Nevertheless, I do think he kept it. If only I knew where. Or, for that matter, why.'

''Course, he was a secretive little man,' said Kate. 'If he thought he could use it . . . Against you, for instance. Silly old Sybilla says he wasn't secretive because he was always boasting about those torture games he played. But he was. He liked gloating over things – having knowledge, enjoying the thought of what he knew. Crackers, if you ask me. Dangerous.'

'So it seems. Still, if it was something that concerned me, that was surely no reason for killing him. Do you think he was the one to pinch the pictures, Aunt Kate?'

'Leo? No. Not the type. No gloaty fun in that. Too risky, too.'

'Who do you think it was?'

'I think old Lawrence popped them himself. Stashed the money away somewhere the Inland Revenue won't find it. For the Squealies. Or else it was Peter, and Lawrence is covering up for him. Or McWatters.'

'That's three,' I pointed out. 'Which do you really think took them?'

'McWatters knows Iti,' said Kate. 'Bit suspicious, what? Ever heard of a butler who knew Iti before? Must be an art buff, or something.'

'How did you know that he knows Italian, by the way, Aunt? Is he open about it? Did you all know?'

'Don't suppose the rest knew. Not interested, except in keeping him. I get around the house a bit. Trailing. Heard him talking one evening to Mrs Mac. Maria-Luisa had been shouting insults at us over dinner. Does that periodically. Comes from the gutter. Scum. *Untermensch.* Anyway, old McWatters heard 'em all, and was translating them to his missus. Singed my hair, I can tell you!'

'So you'd pick McWatters – getting in with the house-hold and progressively robbing it of pictures?'

'Makes sense. Rather have that than one of the family.'

I sighed. That was no argument. Aunt Kate was not the logical thinker of the family. I put down my fork with every appearance of regret, leaving a little mountain of food as if I thought it the polite thing to do, and stood up.

'Well, I'd better be getting back to work, Aunt Kate,' I said.

Unluckily her eyes were on the level with my waist, and she peered disapprovingly at the bulge in my trousers.

'Shouldn't stuff things in your pockets like that, Perry,' she said. 'You young people don't know how to treat good clothes!'

'Er, is there anything else, Aunt Kate?' I said hurriedly, 'anything else you would like to tell me?'

She was still chomping away, unwilling to miss a mouth-ful, but she became pensive and finally she said: 'Don't know if you realize how much we hated Leo. Well, we did. We didn't have rows with him, but we all hated him. He got to our weak points and he twisted the knife in. We're all failures in a way, him most of all. But he made us all feel it. He made us squirm.'

'He certainly made me squirm.'

'You were just a boy. It's different when you're old. Worse. He was a man who would have hated to be loved. Because he couldn't love. Think of your poor mother. He despised her. Ignored her. Even you children. He hadn't an ounce of feeling for you. And you were a lovely little boy, Perry! Golly, you were nice!'

I blushed purple.

'But he hated you by the end, and he'd have done anything to spite you. He tolerated Chris because she looked after him, but he despised her too, and he'd have made her life hell when he found out about the baby. He was a *horrible* little twerp, Perry! You can't expect any of us to feel sorry he's gone.'

131

'I don't,' I said. 'Even Chris, I don't think—'

'Oh, Chris, underneath, doesn't care. And she'll have the baby now. It'll be better for her, you know, when she has that to look after.'

'I know. But I wish she could have been married. Chris is the sort that ought to get married. And it'll be much worse with him in the same house. That I do feel bitter about. Of course I know things aren't easy for him either. Without a proper job, and no outlets . . .'

Aunt Kate let out a great whoop of laughter. 'No outlets!'

'Well, I don't imagine Morrie has a wildly exciting sex life, stuck here in Harpenden—'

'Oh Perry, you are a chump! It's not Morrie, it's Pete!'

CHAPTER 13

IN WHICH I HAVE AN IDEA

Chump was as good a word as any for it. I had been the most complete and utter chump. I had remembered Cristobel's expression of sympathy for Morrie and jumped obediently to the wrong conclusion. I would have done better to ask myself whose name Cristobel *didn't* mention once during the course of that first interview: Peter's. And what really got me as I strode through the house and up to my bedroom was that when I had talked to her a couple of hours before she had known I had fixed on Morrie as the father, and she'd let me go on thinking it. Worse, I had the feeling that she'd been playing with me, like an angler with a big and not very bright fish, ever since I arrived. We had been too dismissive of Cristobel's intellect. She clearly had depths of animal cunning I had never hitherto plumbed.

What was still more worrying was the feeling that she was quite simply holding back on me. That she knew something she was not telling. Knew what had been going on in this house, but for some reason or other – and I could think of some – was keeping mum. I didn't like that. It was foolish, it was unsisterly, it was dangerous. One thing I was quite sure of: there had been a letter to me, and Chris knew about it. Why else hold back on the subject of her own letter from our mother? Something she had, according to Kate, burbled on about quite happily at the time she received it. The fact was, she must only recently have found out about my letter. Somehow found it and read it. And my letter, from Chris's point of view, was obviously a hot potato.

When I got to my stateroom, I flushed the little pile of risotto from my bag down the lavatory, and cleaned my teeth vigorously to get the taste of Aunt Kate's efforts out of my mouth. Then I went over to the desk, to the notebooks that had been sitting there since the night I arrived, and I scrawled 'Peter, Peter, Peter – damn him!' all over a new blank page. That relieved my feelings a bit. I sat down with the intention of being more rational, and I wrote: 'Pregnancy – significant, or just carelessness?' And then I asked: 'Did Cristobel tell Father?'

But no train of thought could bring Cristobel's pregnancy from being a side issue to occupying the centre of the stage. I could not see how the answer to the murder could lie there. I was just about to put down a query on the baffling subject of the letter and its whereabouts when I glanced out of the window and saw Jan and Daniel being shown around the grounds by Sybilla and Mordred. They were near the tree where two nights before I had stood watching Maria-Luisa launch her marital missile, and they started off down towards the lake. Well, it was a lovely afternoon, and the fact is, I couldn't resist. Damn the case, I thought: they're my family. (Ignoring the fact that so was the case.) I went out to them.

Daniel – we seldom call him Dan, by the way, because Jan and Dan sounds like some ghastly cartoon film, with people who talk in funny voices – Daniel was capering around, beside himself with delight. The Trethowans went tremendously up in his estimation for owning such an enormous expanse of ground. And I could see his point. It was a pretty good feeling to know you could get all the exercise you could possibly need without danger from cars or muggers, and without passing beyond the confines of your own domain.

'Daddy! Daddy!' Daniel screamed as I came up. 'I can run for miles and miles and not have to turn round!'

And he suited action to words. I strolled up to the little

sightseeing party – Jan all modest and a-watch, like Elizabeth Bennet being shown over Pemberley – and I greeted the others and put my arm around Jan.

'He loves the space,' she said.

'Children do,' said Sybilla.

'You like space too, Perry,' said Jan.

'Of course he does,' said Sybilla. 'He grew up here.'

I was beginning to get a nasty feeling of being accepted back in the fold.

'Don't the Squealies ever get out into the open?' I asked.

'Sometimes,' said Sybilla, with a downward curve of her discontented mouth. 'Sometimes they're locked in the tennis court. But the eldest are beginning to be able to climb the fence. Today they're all at the dentist.'

'Poor things!' I said. 'I mean the dental people.'

'They have to go to a new one each time. They're known over a wide radius, and they're having to be taken further and further afield. Luckily their mother cuts their hair herself. Now *this*, Jan, is the lake.' (I have commented before on Sybilla's capacity to state the obvious.) 'This is the lake Perry threw Mordred into in the year 'fifty-eight. It was over there . . .'

As Sybilla seemed about to expatiate on this not-very-interesting topic, and still seemed to nurse a motherly sense of outrage, I took Morrie aside.

'Mordred, I'm sorry—'

'Oh, for heaven's sake, Perry. It was twenty years ago.'

'Not for throwing you in, you ass. Since I was ten and you were sixteen I'm rather proud of it. For snapping at you this morning. The fact is, I'd got the idea that you'd done something, and now I find you hadn't.'

'Oh? Denuding the family picture collection?'

'No – making my sister pregnant.'

'Is she pregnant? That would be Pete.'

'Yes,' I said grimly. 'That would be Pete. Did they make it that obvious?'

'Not at all. At least, I never noticed anything. It's just

135

that it's the sort of thing he does. Getting people pregnant makes him feel good.'

'Well, if he must scatter his maker's image through the land, I wish he wouldn't do it via my sister,' I said. 'It makes me puke. It's worse than when I thought it was you. Quite apart from anything else, what's Maria-Luisa going to do when she finds out?'

'Hmmm. If I were Chris I certainly would avoid coming to dinner on the nights when she's cooking what my mama calls her delicious Mediterranean specialities. Though in point of fact it's not the first time our little Neapolitan child of nature has had to face news of that kind.'

'Really? Who else?'

'Oh, there was the wife of a filthy-rich Yorkshire industrialist. Then there was the literary editor of the *New Spectator*.'

'So that's how he got the job. Interesting variant on the old-fashioned interview.'

'He likes the sort who are not likely to sue for maintenance. None of your barmaids or local peasant wenches for Pete. He's very calculating when he dips his wick.'

'Peregrine! Mordred!' came the vulturine voice of Aunt Sybilla. 'What are you so deep in converse over? I will not be left out, Peregrine. Tell me all. Have you found those pictures?'

We were at the far edge of the lake, not far from the summerhouse. We stopped, like tourists, to look back at that monstrous house, that heavy load of architectural pretension burdening the strong back of Northumberland.

'Well, actually, yes, Aunt Sybilla,' I said. 'We've found the *Lord Byron*, anyway. It's been . . . at any rate acquired, probably bought, by Newstead Abbey.'

Sybilla was ecstatic. 'You see! You hear that, Mordred? I was right. You've all been mocking me, saying things weren't *really* missing—'

'Half of them were *found*, Mother dear,' said Mordred.

'*Put back*! I was right all along. Somebody is dissipating the family heritage. Peregrine, I really think you have been *quite* clever. It may be we have been misjudging you a teeny bit all these years. So appropriate, too! What a Trethowan has dispersed, a Trethowan recovers!'

'Well, we're not sure of the legal—'

'We shall demand it back. Of course. Now, perhaps if you've seen enough of the garden, Janet, we could go into the summerhouse and Peregrine can tell us *all*.'

But I didn't want that. I wasn't going to be a police mole, feeding the gutter press through Aunt Sybilla. Besides, I had seen through the thick skirting of shrubs a scrap of blue material in the summerhouse, telling me that Chris was there (she loves that sort of middling blue that suggests nothing so much as one of the Women's services). Presumably she had not left the place since we spoke, or else had come back. Perhaps it had memories of a sentimental or erotic nature for her. Luckily the rest of the party was headed off by Daniel, who was gazing at the modified jungle stretching for miles beyond the lake in the direction of Thornwick and demanding (in a rather grand-seigneurial voice, I thought): 'But I want to see it all!'

Sybilla rather reluctantly consented. 'Perhaps we could go a little further. He is really rather a *nice* boy, yours, Peregrine.'

Of course I agreed. But with the current standards of comparison available to Sybilla, it was a bit like winning a gold at the Moscow Olympics. Jan obviously had not yet exhausted her curiosity any more than Daniel had, so I let them go off quite happily through the undergrowth and made my way over to the summerhouse. I was not welcome. As soon as Chris saw me she set her face in an obstinate line.

'Go *away*, Perry. You're hounding me. You promised you wouldn't. I will *not* talk to you.'

'Very well, then, I'll talk to you, Chris,' I said, sitting down beside her. 'First of all, let me say I've been an absolute fool about the father of your baby, but you must admit you led me on.' She looked mulish and kept her mouth shut. 'Now I know it's Pete, and of course that

137

makes it much worse. Chris, you must leave this place. Adding another Squealy to the pack is really carrying wildlife preservation a bit far. Think of the fuss Maria-Luisa is going to make, and I can't say I blame her. I thought you might want to stick around in the hope that he'd marry you, but now of course there's no question of that—'

'Who says there's no question?' Cristobel burst out. 'There's such a thing as divorce.'

'Has that come up? Has he said he wants to marry you?'

'He said wouldn't it be wonderful if we could . . .'

Oh, my God! Don't they teach you *anything* in the Guides? I held my temper with great difficulty.

'Right. That's the first thing I've at last got straight in my mind. Now for the second. You received a letter, Chris, from Mother, sent by her lawyers, I'd guess on your twenty-first birthday.' She looked obstinate, but shifty. She also looked scared of what was coming. 'I think it very unlikely that Mother, when she was dying, would have written a last letter to you, but not one to me. I believe that a similar letter had also been sent to me, earlier, on my twenty-first birthday. It must have been sent by the lawyers to this house, where it was intercepted by Father – out of spite, or for some other reason. He could have destroyed it, but I don't believe he did. Chris, I think you know of this letter, and I think you know where it is.'

'You're talking in riddles,' said Chris shortly. 'I've never heard of any letters.'

'Chris, don't be entirely dim. When you got yours you went around talking about it to people. Naturally. Everyone in the house knows you got it. I've only got to get on the phone to Mother's lawyers to confirm it.'

'I don't know anything about any letter to you.'

'I think you do. That's why you lied about receiving one yourself. You knew I'd wonder why she hadn't written to me too. Chris: she was our mother. We both loved her.

138

I've got a right to know what she wrote to me. How would you feel if yours had been kept from you? Where is it, Chris?'

I could see that I had got to her. She had flinched when I spoke. But still she remained obstinately dumb.

'Chris, what do the letters WOAF mean?'

'I think they're some kind of United Nations organization.'

'God in heaven, Chris — Father didn't send our mother's letter to a United Nations agency! Come on: tell me what it means.'

But she would say nothing, and sat there obstinately looking ahead of her, her eyes wet but determined. When she gets that Christian martyr look on her there's nothing can shift Chris. I spent a few minutes battering away at her silence, like waves on Beachy Head, but after a bit I had to give up. I stormed off. But it's not very satisfying to shout 'You haven't heard the last of this!' when you know you've been well and truly worsted.

I suppose it was this feeling of frustration that made me open up to the McWatterses when I found them in the hall. They were puzzling over a pile of wreaths that for some reason had been sent to the house. As it was by no means clear when my revered father ('An Ornament to British Music' as one of the wreath-cards put it) would be consigned to the earth, it was difficult to know what to do with them. Finally we decided to ring the family undertaker and get him to come and take them away. But when we'd done that we stood around in the hall for a bit, chewing the cud. McWatters was gently, courteously amused by the whole business, Mrs McWatters was displaying what is usually called a grim relish for the misfortunes of Harpenden.

'Did either of you know,' I asked, deciding this was one family secret it was quite useless to hide from the domestics, 'that my sister was pregnant?'

They looked at each other. 'Hmmm,' said Mrs McWatters. 'We had an idea that Something was Up.'

'The summerhouse,' said McWatters roguishly, 'was

becoming more popular than its attractions seemed to justify. Even in summer.'

'I see. I guessed they might have met there. Do you think my father knew about it?'

'I'd take a wee bet – were I a betting man, which I am not – that he'd be among the last to hear. There was not much confidence between the young leddy and her father, particularly not in recent weeks.'

'McWatters, Mrs McWatters, you can be frank with me: I really don't count as a member of the family anymore. You must have overheard a lot of things in the family—'

'Oh, aye,' said McWatters.

'Mek your hair currrl,' said Mrs Mac, descending practically into the bass clef.

'Always something going on,' said McWatters. 'And us being the only regular staff, not counting the leddies who came by day, we heard a goodly lot of it. I've often said to ma wife that a good book could be made of it. But my tastes run more to the visual arrts. And my wife's religion teaches her to disapprove of fiction as lies.'

'Then *what*,' I said, 'was going on in the weeks before my father died?'

McWatters shook his head regretfully. 'I get your drift, sirr, but as I had to tell the other policeman, I don't rightly know. There was something, right enough. Of course, there was the wee matter of the pictures – you've heard about the pictures, I believe?'

'Aye,' I said. 'Yes. Who would you think took them?'

'We-e-ll,' said McWatters, 'I wouldna' mek accusations, but talking it over, the two of us, we cam' to the conclusion that, psychologically speaking—'

'It was Master Peter!' said his wife triumphantly. 'Not a scruple in his body! As your puir sister has no doubt found out!'

'I'm not quite sure she's faced up to that discovery yet,' I said. 'But you don't think the pictures were the root of the trouble?'

'Naw, I do not. Because the pictures thing had begun to blow over. But your late father – God rest his soul, but I ha' ma doots – certainly had something on. He was all excited. Pleased as a cock sparrow wi' himself, he was. He got like that, periodically as you might say. Chuffed was the word we used to use in the army. And he was chuffed in those last few days before his life was terrminated. But *why* he was chuffed, we havena' been able to put a finger on.'

'You say this happened periodically?'

'Aye. Just now and then. It was a real mystery to us. I'll not be denying we were itching to find out. Natural human curiosity, you might say. But it was no go.'

I sighed. 'Ah well. I suppose neither of you would know anything about a letter my mother wrote to me – wrote before she died, to be given to me when I grew up?'

They shook their heads regretfully. 'It's a good old-fashioned notion, that,' said Mrs McWatters. 'But it would be well before our time, wouldn't it?'

'Yes, it would. Well, never mind—'

'Ye'll excuse my asking, sir, but is there anything actually found out about the pictures?'

'Yes. One of them has definitely been located.'

'Ye'll understand, it's been a mite awkward, since the discovery that they were missing. They've been looking a mite askance, both at my leddy wife and maself. The firrst thing they think of is that the staff is thievin'.'

'I'm sure, McWatters, they trust you absolutely.'

'I'm no' so sure about that. We've had some experiences, ma wife and I, in a previous situation. We were accused by a noble lord of stealing his silver, when we knew his wife was pawning it to spend on immorrral purrposes I would na' like to put a name to. So we've been conscious that there's been talk, that we've been regarrded with the eye of suspicion . . .'

'I think you can be sure that the picture business at least will be cleared up in a day or two,' I said. I added (though I was not sure they really minded being suspected, but really rather enjoyed contemplating the bottomless depravity of the Trethowan mind): 'You mustn't take it too hard, if the family did for a moment wonder . . . After all, living in a disorganized house like this, full of valuable paintings, it wouldn't be surprising if you'd felt the temptation . . .'

'You think so, sir? Pairsonally, since my time in Italy I've never fancied anything later than the Rococo.'

And, conscious that he had said something that was unlikely to be capped, McWatters led his leddy wife back to the servants' quarters. I slowly made my way up that long flight of stairs, so wide and so lonely-making – I always felt like the sole person in some megalomaniac's private opera-house when I walked them. In my bedroom the notebooks and the questions remained, looking reproachfully at me for my dereliction of duty. All the old questions were there, unanswered – or, if I had some provisional answers in my mind, they needed that corner-stone, the establishment of motive, before they could be brought out into the daylight. I wrote:

'Why has Chris been lying?'

and I put down some possible answers: 'to protect herself?' 'to protect her inheritance?' 'to protect Peter?' 'to protect me???'

I had seen when I spoke to her that last time that the only thing that really got through to her was when I spoke of our mother, of my right to know what she had wanted to say to me, to tell me. Chris is like that: she's the sort of person who can only be appealed to on a direct, close, personal level. Larger issues, abstractions, mean nothing to her. Such concepts as Justice are meaningless to her, but the bond between mother and child is the sort of thing that goes straight to her heart. Still, she had resisted it, stuck it out obstinately, and no doubt now she was strengthening her fortifications against future attack.

And the thing was, in a sense, urgent. If Chris knew

where the letter was, she could destroy it. Not, probably, while there were policemen all over the house – and certainly not if, as seemed likely, it was hidden somewhere in the Gothic wing. But when they moved out, and things began to return to normal, then she could get at it again, and then she might simply burn it. I didn't want that. Not just for the sake of the case. I did want to know what my mother had written to me. I smiled sadly as I thought of her – poor, pale, ill-adapted creature, lying on that sofa, perhaps, and penning some preposterous injunctions totally out of tune with the world of the 'sixties and 'seventies that I in fact grew up into. No doubt it was something along the lines of Christina's dying letter in *The Way of All Flesh*, which I had read as a boy, and taken seriously, been moved to tears by. A child could not see the deadly irony behind the letter, anymore than he could see the way Christina's egotistical fantasizings were laid bare. But I didn't think my mother's letter would be like Christina's. She might well have been a fantasist, but unless my childish perceptions were totally awry she had none of the egotism of poor Butler's parents whom he so joyously delivered over to public crucifixion. Butler was a very special case, even if he did regard it as the way of all . . .

The Way of All Flesh! Oh my God, what a fool I'd been! WOAF! Just like my father's sense of humour, to hide it snuggled next to Christina's letter. The obvious had been staring me in the face – throwing itself at me only yesterday as I sat in the library, remembering. And I hadn't tumbled to it, even when I looked along the shelves. I jumped up, dashed from the room, and took those gloomy corridors as if I were pacemaker for Steve Ovett. I was down the stairs three at a time and then through the corridors to the Gothic wing like a flash.

'I've had an idea!' I bellowed to PC Smith as he tried to bar my way.

I raced up to the library and stood there looking distractedly

143

along the Thackerays, the Dickenses and the George Eliots. There it was, Butler. First edition of 1903. I pulled it down, and as I held it in my hands it fell open at Chapter 25, at Christina's very letter.

But the letter from my mother, which had been there, was gone.

CHAPTER 14

IN WHICH I HAVE ANOTHER IDEA

It was a blow, but when I thought about it I felt pretty sure I knew what had happened, though I hadn't a scrap of evidence to prove it. The letter had been there, and it had been filched by Chris. She had heard about it, or perhaps she had seen father gloating over it, had investigated, found it and read it. Then she had taken it. *Why?* I did not know, but I did feel gut-sure she had taken it.

I sat there, on the arm of the library sofa, looking at the volume of Butler open at Christina's letter to Ernest. Suddenly an extremely interesting idea occurred to me. Was it not conceivable, in fact, that Cristobel had taken it on the very night of the murder? She had talked that first time about coming down to get aspirin because she couldn't sleep. She had hesitated when she said it. It was possible that the reason she couldn't sleep was connected with her pregnancy, and hence the hesitation. But it was surely equally possible that she had lain in bed, meditating some decisive action in the matter of the letter; that she had come down to the first floor, got the letter from Butler, and then – what? Destroyed it? But how? There had certainly been no fires in the Gothic wing on the day of the murder. The police had moved in on the same night, and since then nothing had been altered. The grates were perfectly clean. If paper had been burned with matches or a lighter, the police would have picked up traces of it, in ashtray or dustbin. And if she was desperate to destroy it, Chris would certainly not regard tearing up as final enough.

She *must*, surely, have hidden it again — if only as a prelude to a more final destruction. And then she had heard, from downstairs, the sound of the machine going . . . On top of the tension involved in the stealing of the letter, it was no wonder the finding of our father had led Chris to her monumental bout of hysterics. The wonder is she didn't miscarry on the spot.

There was only one speck of light in the situation as I saw it: this was that *since* those hysterics, Chris had not set foot in the wing, and could be prevented from doing so now. If necessary we could draft a whole posse of constables from the army currently infesting the house and get them to take the Gothic wing apart. I didn't want that. There was nothing much here I would grieve for, except the books of my childhood, but since the place was now Chris's I did hope it could be prevented. I know what a thorough police search can do to a place.

It was difficult to know what to do next, but as a precaution I went down to warn PC Smith, on the door, that he was to enforce the strictest of bans on *anybody* unauthorized coming into the Gothic wing, and that the main door was to be guarded twenty-four hours a day. No doubt this was in any case supposed to be the rule, but Lawrence's gardeners had got in, no doubt during one of PC Smith's trips to the loo, or to get a bite to eat, and it would do no harm to underline the orders as heavily as I knew how. It was odd, giving orders to PC Smith, who had chased me out of orchards in my youth. I reflected that if I'd tried to join the police at the time I'd left home, and if they'd contacted him, he would probably have told them that I was a young tearaway and not at all the type they were after. PC Smith was not of the brightest, and would probably never have understood my need to break out after my dreary childhood at and around my mother's death-bed.

'What's going on in there?' I said, to break the ice a bit after I'd laid down the law, and jerking my head in the direction of the Torture Chamber.

'Him as made that there Indian rope trick arrangement,' said PC Smith. 'The Superintendent phoned him, and he turned up half an hour ago, bold as brass and twice as cocky.'

'*Really*?' I said. 'He wasn't a furtive little man in a mac, then?'

'No, sir,' said Smith, bewildered. 'Sun's shining today, sir.'

'So it is. Well, I'd better go in and have a look at him. After all, he's the one who made all this possible.'

'Quite an *ordinary*-looking chap,' said PC Smith, as if deeply disappointed.

And he was right. Mr Ramsay Percival was a sharp, jolly little man, running to fat and to baldness, but with a chirpy manner that even his presence in the same room as his ropey contraption could not dampen.

'Well, well, you must be Mr Peregrine, the poor old fellow's son,' he said, getting up from his chair on the wrong side of Tim Hamnet's improvised desk and coming over with his hand outstretched. I took it. It's not often you get the chance of shaking hands with the man who's indirectly killed your father.

'How did you know?'

'Your name? It's in all the papers,' he said. 'Big Perry. Picture in the *Northerner*. Your aunt says you have a razor-sharp mind like all the Trethowans. She's a genius, that old bird. Marvellous story this is making. Shouldn't wonder if it doesn't prove a real gold-mine for me.'

'I shouldn't wonder either,' I said. 'Do you have a wide circle of clients, or were you living off my father?'

'By no means. I do very nicely — keep myself busy, which is as much as anybody wants, isn't it? Of course, I could expand, but at my time of life who wants to become a tycoon?'

'Tell me,' I said, gesturing him back into the chair and coming over to stand by Tim, 'how you came to go into this line of business.'

'Just what I was about to tell the Super here,' he said

cheerily, deciding to sit on the corner of the desk. 'Well, three or four years ago, I got the sack. Made redundant, they called it, but it didn't take the sting out of it. Getting the sack is pretty much of a facer when you're pushing fifty, I can tell you. Doesn't give you much to look forward to in the years before you start to pick up your pension. Now, I've always been a handy, inventive sort of chap, all my life. Now and then I'd knocked up a few little things for my friends. Ingenious little devices of one sort or another, you know. Well, I started picking up the odd bit of extra like that, supplementing the dole, like. Now, one day I was in the local — the Earl Grey in Edward Short Street — and I was telling some blokes about this sprinkler thing I'd made for my mate's garden — smart little thing, it was, that moved itself round automatically and watered the whole garden while he was at work. Well now, the next time I goes to the bar for a refill, this chap comes up to me—'

'Leo Trethowan?' asked Hamnet.

'No, no. Not in the Earl Grey in Edward Short Street. No, well, this chap — I won't tell you his name — came up to me, asked if he could buy me a drink. He took me away into a corner and asked if I was interested in doing a job for him. The fact was, it was a little pain-giving thing called Pain Forty Dure, if you'll pardon my French. Don't know if you've heard of it, you gents?' He looked round at us cheerily. We looked noncommittal, and he seemed disappointed in us.

'Well, he was a nice bloke, kink apart, and when I'd made the thing, and given every satisfaction, he said, why didn't I try it for a living? He suggested I put an ad in one or two of the S-and-M and fladge publications. Well, I wasn't too sure what he meant — and thought it might be some kind of trade publication. But I got him to do it for me, and quite frankly, I've never looked back. Always something new to test my ingenuity, some little quirk or oddity to be catered for, and that's what makes it such a satisfying profession.'

He looked round at us again, with an expression of enormous self-approbation.

'Now, I don't know about you gents, but I regard that as a success story. Just the sort of enterprise and initiative that Old Mother Thatcher is always recommending: the small, independent bloke finding where the trade is, and going out and getting it. As she said in Parliament the other day, the work is there, if people are only willing to seek it out. I should get a Queen's Award to Industry, by rights.'

'So Mr Trethowan got in touch with you as a consequence of the advertisement, did he?' asked Tim.

'That's it. Talked it over on the phone, I dropped over and had a peep at the room, and Bob's your uncle. When he died, I was working on a rack for him – nice little job, it's over there, you see. He had it on appro, to see how it worked. I was expecting a nice little succession of jobs from Mr Trethowan. Still, the great thing about this trade is, the market never dries up. You're not going to get people's kinks suddenly ironed out, are you? Soon as you lose one, there's another anxious and waiting to take his place. I'd go into exporting if I had the time. I believe Japan's got a marvellous market for things of this kind.'

'You got a fair whack out of Mr Trethowan for this, I see,' said Tim.

'Naturally I did. I always do. They're paying me for my inventive skills, remember. And it's not the kind of thing you can patent and protect yourself on. I must say, in all fairness, the gentlemen with this sort of interest, they're very generous gentlemen. They're a good class, that's what it is: public school, often as not. Very seldom a quibble, which is nice when you're in trade. Keeps it on a genteel sort of basis. The fact is, they appreciate craftsmanship, and they're willing to pay for it.'

'You're not worried by any moral scruples about what you're doing?'

'Good Lord, no. Why would I be? The market's there, and all I do is move in and supply it.'

'Pretty much like a pornographer, eh?'

'That's it. You've hit the nail on the head. In principle it is very much the same sort of thing, and pornography, as you gentlemen know, is perfectly legal these days, especially when published and marketed with the full knowledge and co-operation of the police.'

'Trethowan was pushing seventy,' said Tim. 'You realize you could easily kill yourself with one of these devices?'

' 'Course you could,' said Mr Percival. 'Same as you can on top of a Mayfair tart. If that's the way you choose to go, what business is it of anybody else's? That's what freedom is all about – we're trying to stop the State prying into every aspect of people's lives, aren't we? And the fact is, as you very well know, Mr Leo – God rest his soul in peace, if that's what he wants – would be here today if someone hadn't slipped in and snipped that cord. He was a gentleman who knew how to enjoy his pleasures *and* take care of himself at the same time. He knew exactly when he'd gone far enough. Enjoyed life, Mr Leo did, without endangering himself.'

'You talk,' I said, 'as if we ought to thank you for making the last years of my father's life full and happy ones.'

'Exactly,' said Mr Percival. 'Very nicely put, and I appreciate the thought.'

Nothing, clearly, was going to discompose Ramsay Percival.

'I've been wondering,' I said, looking up at the deployment of ropes and pulleys stretching up to the ceiling, 'where this machine would be best heard from upstairs, when it was going.' Tim looked at me sharply, so he had obviously had the same thought. 'Do you think we could set it going?'

'Nothing easier!' said Mr Percival, with professional pride.

'What we really need,' I said, 'is someone strapped into it. Otherwise the machine won't strain as it ought to do, and we won't hear anything. You wouldn't like to oblige yourself, Mr Percival?'

'Here! Come off it! I'm normal! I'm old-fashioned – I go for girls. I never try out my own inventions. It'd be like a bespoke tailor trying his suits on himself.'

'What a pity. I was looking forward to that. Do you think you could try your circus act again, Tim?'

'Oh – been trying it out for yourselves, have you, gentlemen?' said the irrepressible Mr Percival. 'Now, if ever you wanted anything special made for the Yard, I'd be happy to oblige.'

'No chance, I'm afraid,' I said. 'We use the electrodes plugged into the genitals at headquarters. The march of progress, you know. Tim, give me two minutes, will you, and then start it up. Twice will be enough.'

'It will bloody well have to be,' said Tim.

I ran up the stairs again, and went first to the little kitchen where Chris had said she had gone to get the aspirin. It was on the wrong side of the wing, and, as I had suspected, nothing could be heard of the working of the machine from there. So she'd lied about that. Neither could it from the little sitting-room, which had once been my mother's room. When I moved to the library, a dull sound as of distant jets could be heard if one was exceptionally attentive. It was only when I moved into the study that the noise could be heard at all well. So far so good. I moved around the room, trying to find the point of maximum audibility. It was, in fact, a yard or so from the fireplace. This, presumably, was the point just over the upper pulley, up to which my father (or currently Tim) was being hauled. It was a fair bet that it was around here somewhere that Chris first noticed the noise.

I stood there, looking around me. Had Chris been standing here on Thursday night, looking for a place of concealment? Was she then suddenly struck by the gruesome noise below, forced into the realization that her father was not in bed, but was still being hauled up and down on his appalling machine? But whatever happened, she must have hidden it. Must have made a sudden decision what to do with it, then hurried down to see what was up in the Torture Chamber. Because she certainly didn't take the letter with her on her raving hysterics over the house, wearing only her nightdress. Where, then?

And as I stood there, looking at the fireplace and the Dali over it, I remembered telling Chris about Lawrence sending the outdoors men to take it away. She had said 'The Dali!', with a catch in her voice. Then it came back to me that the night before, when Lawrence had gone on and on about retrieving 'his' property, Chris had immediately chimed in with the claim that Father had assured her that the Dali was his, that he had bought it himself. Now the claim was patently absurd. The Dali had been bought in the late 'twenties, was a product of his Paris period. At that time my father was a student at the Guildhall School, had inherited nothing from his father, and was certainly in no position to purchase young but fashionable painters. I had assumed that the lying claim was Leo's, which Chris had not seen through. But what if it was Chris's – and prompted not by a desire to assert her claims on portable property, but because she had hidden the letter there?

I went over and took it down from the wall. At least it was the sort of picture you *could* lift from the wall, unlike the John Martin in my bedroom. I laid it on the floor and inspected the back. Yes – a narrow slit had been made there, and inside . . . I eased my fingers into the slit, and caught a glimpse of blue paper. I enlarged the slit, and drew out a long envelope. It was ladies' notepaper, 'fifties style – a blue, padded envelope such as I remembered my mother using. I turned it over. It was addressed: 'To my dear son Peregrine Trethowan'.

I got out of that hated study, my father's own room, and went through to the library, where I had spent so many childhood hours to be within call of my mother. I sat down on the sofa, and took out of the envelope four small sheets covered with my mother's thin, angular handwriting – the writing I remembered so well from her letters to me when she travelled abroad for her health. For a moment I could hardly bear to unfold the sheets: they seemed addressed to another person – a quiet, lonely child, haunting a gloomy house.

Finally I took my courage into my hands and opened it. It was dated March 21st, 1958 – about two months before my mother's death. I read:

> My darling Perry,
>   When you read this, I shall be dead – and so long dead, I suppose, that you will have forgotten me, have only dim memories of what I looked like, what I sounded like.

No Mother. I remember. I remember very well. I can hear you now.

> I know that I was a poor mother to you, Perry, and to Cristobel. And especially that I could do so little for a strong, healthy boy like you. But something in me hopes that you will have some remembrances of me, and retain a little from our talks together. Above all, I know that you will always have done your duty as a brother, and looked after little Cristobel, as you faithfully promised.

That really got me, and I broke down, bawling unashamedly, feeling more feeble and inadequate than I had felt, perhaps, since the day my mother died. A fine one I had been, to have been entrusted with the care of Cristobel. A fine job I had made of it.

> I don't think [my mother wrote] that there is any last message I can give you that will help you in any way in life. It is not for the dying and the failed to try to do this. I feel confident, Perry, that you, who are a determined little boy, will make your way in life creditably and successfully.

It is because I know that you will grow up steel-straight and with a heart full of honour—

And I cried again, at the G. A. Henty sentiments and the Freudian imagery, and the absurdity of imagining anyone of my generation growing up with a heart full of honour.

—that I entrust to you the following facts, to act on as you see fit. You see, I believe I know you, and I believe that when you are a man you will know the *right*, and the *upright*, thing to do. I wish I did myself – wish I did not have to rely on you to make a decision I am unable to make myself, but I feel totally incapable of action. You see, I am depending entirely on your judgment of what a gentleman's duty is.

Last year I went, you will remember, on a cruise in search of the health that has eluded me for many years. Alas, it was of no avail, but that is not the point now. I went, you may remember, around the world, on the *Stratheden*. When the ship docked at Sydney and began the return voyage via the Panama Canal, there came to the next table from my own a Mrs Trethowan. She was very vulgar, and jolly, and familiar, and tried to scrape up an acquaintance on the basis of our names. No, on re-reading this I think I am being unfair. I have no reason to think she was not what people call a 'good-sort', but you know how tongue-tied I am, and how difficult it is for me to talk easily to those who are not of our own sort. She was Irish by birth, an East Londoner by upbringing, and had lived in Sydney for more than twenty years. She kept a hat shop there. I confess, I tried to avoid her, to freeze her off. However, one day, when the boat was in the South Seas, she sat herself down beside me on deck, and insisted on confiding her life-story to me. And to my horror it became clear that she was Florence Trethowan – 'Flo' as he always called her, when he spoke of her at all – the first wife of your Uncle

154

Lawrence, who according to him had died long ago, before the Second War. I couldn't believe my ears at first, but there could be no doubt about it: she had been to Harpenden, briefly; had lived with Lawrence in London for a few years in the early 'twenties; had brought up his son Wallace who died at Arnhem. The frightful thing was, that when she talked of Lawrence – in a sadly bold and indiscreet way – she always referred to him as 'my husband', and announced more than once: 'I'm a Catholic. I don't believe in divorce. He wanted one, but I refused point-blank. He'll have to wait till I'm pushing up the daisies before he gets spliced again, and I'm not going to pop off in a hurry.' She talked like that. It was quite frightful. So frightful that when she asked me about my family, I told a lie – the first one that came into my head: that we came from Cornwall. After a time, thank Heaven, she gave me up, and found friends more to her own taste and of her own class.

Perry, my darling, I have worried and worried over this, and have come to the conclusion about what is right. Of course you will see at once how this affects you. It affects your father too, as you must realize, but for various reasons, and because it could probably only be of consequence to him *very late in his life*, I prefer to confide the matter to you, leaving it to your judgment as a *man*, and as a Christian, as well as a member of a family which, to be fair, one must say has made its mark in the world. It is you who must decide whether this matter should be brought out into the light, with all the consequences that must flow from this. I am happy to die in the serene knowledge that you will take the *honourable* as well as the gentlemanly course.

And now, Perry, it is time to say goodbye.

Your very loving
Mother.

And I sat there in the library, and cried and cried. And laughed too, now and then, through my tears. Did my mother think she was presenting me with a delicate test of my honour, a nicely balanced ethical problem? Did she think of Harpenden House and the headship of the Trethowan family as an inducement? A prize to be won? A shimmering gold light at the end of the tunnel? How little she foresaw! I should have no qualm about renouncing the throne of the Trethowans. The problem was, how was it to be done.

CHAPTER 15

A CONCENTRATION OF NIGHTMARES

I calmed down after a bit. I took out a handkerchief, blew my nose and wiped my eyes, and sat on in the library, wondering what the hell I was going to do.

Not about Harpenden and the heirship of the Trethowans, of course. That was a poisoned chalice I had no difficulty in repulsing. Even my mother, underneath, had wanted me to reject it. That much, on looking the letter over again, it was possible to read between the lines. I wished my motives were as pure and upright as my mother would have desired. Still, I had the feeling that she too did not think the Trethowans much of a family to be head of.

But the question remained: how was I to do it? How was the information in my mother's letter to be kept secret? Because the news that I was the 'rightful heir' (Oh God! How that brought back Jan's and my laughing over whether I or Peter was the Young Master!) was a vital piece, the last vital piece, in the case against the murderer of my father. And as soon as I revealed it to the police – to the *other* police, that is: I must never forget that I was part of them – the information was open, public, never more to be concealed. To tell the family was one thing. I could see that that would probably have to be done. But to tell the police was to licence them to bring it out in court. And if that happened, I was lost. Loaded on my back would be the burden of Harpenden and the assorted dreadfuls that made up the Trethowan family. Amateur weightlifter I may be, but not even Rakhmanov could bear such a load as that.

One solution, it occurred to me, would be to conceal the letter and let the murderer go unpunished. It was not as though I felt a Hamletish compulsion to avenge the death of my father. The Prince of Denmark could perhaps not take the line that his old man was well out of the way – an awfully long-winded old chap he must have been, though, to judge by his post-morten incursions – but I suffered from no such inhibitions. Nevertheless, there is in a policeman (the old-fashioned policeman, a dying species, like the sperm whale) an instinct that tells him that crime, and of all crimes murder, must not go unpunished. That it, above all, is something that threatens the social fabric, and must be seen to incur society's wrath. Awfully dated stuff, that, but somewhere at the back of my mind it clung. And, quite apart from anything else, who could tell where it might not end? If my father could be killed for the knowledge he acquired from my mother's letter, might not Chris in the course of time likewise fall victim, having the same knowledge? I was not going to compound my ineffectiveness as Chris's protector by virtually conniving at her murder.

It came to me gradually, as I sat there in the mounting gloom, that the only way I might conceivably be safe, safe from the burden of Harpenden, was by staging a confrontation. Even then, a lot would depend on the murderer's reaction. But I was a Trethowan – with disgust and self-loathing I admitted it; at any rate I was Trethowan enough to be fairly confident that I could get inside this murderer's mind, that I could know what his reaction would be. And if I was right, then I would be safe: Tim could do the carting away, and I could in total secrecy tell the family the whole background, make it clear to them that the information was entirely confidential, that I had no intention of acting on it. Then I could bow out of Harpenden. Hey presto, Perry Trethowan, the fabulous escape artist, leaps out of his chains and is a free man again. Curtain and general applause. As long as the information was shared, Chris would be safe, and the atmosphere in the house would not be poisoned by uncertainty and mutual suspicion. Not more than usual, anyway.

I wondered how I would put the matter to Tim. For a start I did not want him in on the confrontation: that would be a lot more effective if it at least *began* as a family powwow, however much the screw might have to be turned later on. Tim could be out there in the hall, but no closer. A bobby in the room always turns any occasion into something as natural and informal as the Sun King's *levée*. And how much should I tell Tim? That answered itself: as much as need be, and no more. On the real motive I would hold back till the bitter end. Not unless the poor chap actually had to prepare a case would I come clean. Tim would surely go along with that if I put a bit of pressure on him. After all, there was other evidence, circumstantial though that might be, to justify a trial confrontation.

I decided to give it a try. But in spite of that it was slowly, and with dragging feet, that I made my way down again to Tim. This was going to be very painful and tricky. It could also prove the decisive few hours of my life.

I had been up there in the library so long, lost in thought, that when I came down Mr Percival had gone about his business, back to his vocation of bringing pain and pleasure to his select little clientele. It was obvious when I opened the door to the Torture Chamber that Tim was pretty pleased with himself. Nothing of interest had been got from Mr Percival, not surprisingly, but one of Tim's underlings had finally got on to the member of the Newstead Board of Trustees who had been mainly involved in the buying of the William Allan.

'Offered for sale by Mr Peter Trethowan,' said Tim triumphantly. 'Fat Pete himself. Sorry, old chap: forgot he was a cousin. All negotiations conducted by him. Naturally they knew his father was still alive, and they asked for his authorization to sell. Which Little Lord Fauntleroy brought them, signed and sealed.'

'Which means—?'

'Either forged, I take it, or obtained when he was having one of his "off days".'

I had my own ideas about that, but I held my peace. I just said: 'Very satisfactory. That's one little loose end neatly tied up.'

'Precisely,' said Tim. 'And it lets your father off that particular hook, if you'll pardon the expression.'

'Yes,' I said. 'He wasn't in on that little game.'

I wondered whether we ought to go further into the question of Peter, whether I ought to inform Tim that, in addition to his other delinquencies, he was also the seducer of my sister. But Chris's pregnancy had not come up, and if she was to be kept out of it, as I fervently hoped would be possible, there was no real need to confide it to Tim at all. So instead I said:

'Tim, do you think we could go over the case as a whole? I've got something to suggest.'

And so we chewed it over, threw it back and forth, and it soon became clear that Tim was on the same road as I was, and pretty much as far along it. Bright boy, Tim. I liked him. So far, so good. I then made my confession that there was one piece of evidence that I was loath to bring forward, for family reasons. I felt a bit of a heel doing it: morally I bamboozled Tim with the old aristocratic family notion (which frankly I don't give a pin for). And I'm afraid he was impressed by it. The great families of this country *did* have their secrets, he seemed to feel. He metaphorically touched his forelock to me. I (mentally) shuffled with embarrassment, and hastened to say that if it became clear that nothing could be done without the evidence I was withholding, I would place it at his disposal like a shot.

I went on, becoming quite eloquent, to put to him the various reasons why I did not think it would be necessary. I began to sell him the idea of a confrontation, a private one, between me and my family, in which the evidence we both had was put before the murderer, fairly, squarely and brutally. I frankly admitted I did not know how it would work out: there might be a confession, there might be blank denial, there might be some other catastrophe. But I didn't see how anything could be lost by it, from our point of view.

Tim was reluctant, at first. He is a cautious chap, as most really good policemen are. There was something flamboyant, a touch of the Dame Agatha, about the whole procedure that he didn't quite take to. But finally, after a burst of my rhetoric and an appeal to him as a comrade, he fell in with the idea. We arranged that I would go down to sherry as usual, and he and a couple of the men would station themselves in the hall, outside the drawing-room door.

'But it's such a hell of a big room, Perry,' said Tim. 'How am I going to hear?'

'Strain your ears,' I said. 'Just strain your bloody ears.'

He shook his head dubiously, and I could see he did not really like it. As I was going out of the door, he said:

'Sure you won't tell me, Perry, what it is you've got hold of?'

And I replied, oozing an agonized sincerity: 'It's a terribly delicate family matter, Tim.'

You bastard, Perry Trethowan. This case was bringing out the lowest I was capable of. Still, I was glad it was Tim that Joe had sent on the case. Glad, too, as it turned out, that Joe had drafted me as well. Think what could have happened if he hadn't. Tim might have come breezing back to the Yard and presented me with the heirship of the Trethowans as if it was the season's biggest win on the Treble Chance.

All this took time. When I got out of the Gothic wing, wiping my forehead with the strain of it, it was already nearly seven. On an impulse I ran upstairs, had a shower, and packed some of my things into my little case. No harm in hoping, after all. With a little bit of luck I could be out of here in a couple of hours. I could spend the night with Jan at the Danby, and drive her back to Newcastle next day. You've no idea how attractive a Sunday in Newcastle can sound when you've been lodged for a few days in a madhouse like Harpenden.

That made it nearly half past. Sherry-time, and hour of decision. I squared my shoulders, told my heart to stop thumping, and marched out of the bedroom. As I walked down the stairs I realized that – clean and showered though I was – the sweat was starting to run. This was it: the decisive coin was spinning in the air, and somehow or other I was going to have to will it to come down heads.

I saw Tim and other dark shapes lurking down one of the corridors. We had arranged that they would not take up their positions until everyone was assembled in the drawing-room. I made no sign to them, but turned at the bottom of the stairs and pushed open the door to the drawing-room.

And there they all were, or most of them, tucking into the sherry. Aunt Sybilla, in one of her most awful drapes, long and magenta, with a heavy amethyst necklace round her scrawny throat. Aunt Kate, in some female equivalent to battle dress. Chris in something frilly and unsuitable. Uncle Lawrence, tucked round with a rug, feeble but assertive. Mordred looking as if drink never passed his lips, but drinking. And there too was Jan, with a self-satisfied, now-I'm-part-of-the-family look on her face. Not for long, my girl, I said to myself grimly. Daniel was standing by her chair, clutching a soft drink, and looking as if this was a very fair substitute for children's television.

A policeman is used to situations where he has, willy-nilly, to take command. But I wanted to start this coolly, so when Uncle Lawrence said in his grand way: 'Sherry, m'boy? Fetch him one, Kate,' I accepted, but coming down to the fireplace (marble, quarried in Carrara or some such place and brought by donkey and steam-train across Europe, to be carved into something infinitely hideous in the North of England) I put my glass down on its absurdly assertive top and turned to them all.

'I wonder,' I said, 'if I might ask something. I thought I ought to have a few words with you all tonight about how the case is going, just to put your minds at rest a bit. If you agree, it might be a good idea if just for this once the Squealies didn't come along.'

'Excellent notion,' said Sybilla.

'Pity to disappoint the little darlings,' said Lawrence.

'Mordred, go along and fetch Peter and Maria-Luisa *alone*,' said Sybilla, flapping a drape.

'Damned woman,' said Lawrence.

'What about Daniel?' asked Mordred, as he made for the door.

'Oh,' I said. 'Perhaps he could go in with the Squealies.'

'No!' said Daniel, with more firmness than I've ever known him muster. So I left him, convincing myself, as adults do, that he would understand very little of what was going on.

I stood there awkwardly, waiting for Peter and Maria-Luisa. I felt Jan's eyes on me: she knew I was up to something. I would very much have preferred her not to be there. Sybilla was sitting snug, pursing her lips with anticipation, wafting her drapes around as if she were part of some ghastly infants' school play. Chris, I noted, was looking mulish. At last the door opened.

'Oh – Pete, Maria-Luisa—' I began.

'What's this? Taken over the family, Perry?' muttered Pete unpleasantly, as they marched in, two mountainous bulges of hostile flesh. And though I hadn't intended it, I suppose it did look a bit as if I'd taken charge.

'I wonder,' I began, now disconcerted, 'if we could put our drinks aside for a moment. This won't take long, but it'll need a bit of concentration.'

Pete, on his way to the drinks tray, glared at me in outraged, puffy dignity, like some Middle-European kingling who has been told by his Prime Minister to give up his favourite mistress.

163

'Who the bloody hell do you think you are?' he asked, and poured doubles for himself and his wife.

Well, eventually they would have to know the answer to that question. For the moment I was just a policeman. I could not restrain myself from throwing him a glance of distaste, but then I drew myself up, saw that the rest had put their glasses by (even, charmingly, Daniel) and were looking at me slightly agape. No doubt about it, they were interested! Time to take the plunge.

'I thought you should know – Uncle Lawrence, Aunt Sybilla, er, all of you – a little about how the case is going. These things take time, and it must seem an eternity to you all already. But we have at least come some way. We seem, for example, to have cleared up one or two side issues, such as the missing pictures—'

'I fail to see,' said Sybilla, looking like a hen who has had her favourite nest-egg snatched from under her, 'how the pictures can be described as a side issue.'

'Nevertheless, they are,' I said. 'Let's ignore them for the moment and concentrate on the main issue: the fact that my father was murdered.'

'Poor old Leo,' said Uncle Lawrence. 'Awful little squirt, but nobody here wished him any harm.'

'No?' I said. 'And yet it's always been difficult for us – us of the police, I mean – to see this as the work of an outsider. It seemed so much more likely that the murderer was someone who knew my father's habits, knew how the machine worked, knew him well enough to break in on him while he was, so to speak, at it. In fact, the first thing that struck me,' I went on, looking around the half-moon of attentive faces, 'almost as soon as I heard of the murder method, was the boldness of it. The aplomb. The theatricality.'

'As a family we are famous for our panache,' said Sybilla, purring.

'Precisely,' I said. 'I think I went a little wrong here, but that *was* one of the things that seemed to me to bring it home here, to Harpenden House. Of course, another way of looking at it might be to say that it was childish. To snip the cord while my father was playing his little sado-masochistic games might in itself seem, to a child, something of a game.' Daniel was about to put in some devastating question, but fortunately he was interrupted by a savage imprecation of a spectacularly southern kind from Maria-Luisa. Uncle Lawrence, too, looked very distressed and muttered: 'Lot of damnable nonsense.'

'Quite,' I said. 'I'm inclined to agree with you. The idea that it was done by the Squealies didn't originate with me. But I noticed that once it was in the air, it spread like wildfire through the house. With the honourable exception of their mother, everyone seems to have thought it a frightfully good idea. It fitted so well. Nobody seems to have reflected that in a sense the Squealies were not the only children in the house.'

'He means me!' said Kate, clapping her hands with glee.

'It was rather the same with the idea of the McWatterses as the thieves of the pictures,' I carried on. 'And I have to admit that the idea occurred to me when I heard he spoke Italian.'

'Well, it did seem *frightfully* suspicious, Perry dear,' said Sybilla, wafting delicately.

'An attractive idea: the art-connoisseur thief, who takes up butling and purloins the family collection. But if that was the case, why did he reveal he spoke Italian after the murder, when he knew the police were on to the question of the missing pictures? He'd always kept quiet about it, and could have gone on doing so. No . . . it didn't add up. It looked to me as if you were all – forgive me – trying to shift the blame from one of the family, or from any member of it likely to be arrested and tried. Perhaps because you knew who had done it. Perhaps because you merely *suspected*.'

'Being a bit long-winded, aren't you, Perry?' said Peter, going back for a refill.

'Yes,' I said. 'But we'll be getting down to brass tacks

in a moment. Now, I mentioned the theatricality of the thing. It seemed, as I say, childish. Perhaps, also, it could have been revengeful. I wondered whether some victim of my father's little kink might not be taking a spectacular revenge − a revenge that would certainly be clear enough to his victim in his last minutes. Uncle Lawrence didn't think there was anybody here that fitted the bill . . .'

'Not *here*,' emphasized Lawrence. 'Could have been someone from London. God knows what he got up to in London.' He licked his lips reminiscently, as of one who has got up to many things in London in his time.

'Once again, an outsider,' I commented.

'Well, why *shouldn't* it be?' burst out Cristobel, with that stupid-obstinate look which irritated me no end still on her face. 'It's perfectly possible. The insurance people have complained about the security here.'

'I think I've made it clear why that's unlikely,' I said. 'In fact, one of the things that really made me rethink my preconceptions about the murder was that, though you're all trying to put the thing on to an outsider, *almost any other* method of murdering my father would have been easier to attribute to an intruder from outside the house. That made me think. Right you are − now we'll get down to the brass tacks, as Peter demanded. When I first came here and started on the case, three things struck me at once.' I looked at them hard, and counted the things off on my fingers. 'One: almost any other method of killing would have been *safer*. Two: granted that it had to be done this way, why was the cord *snipped*, and at that height? Three: why were the lights not switched off? And to these questions I later added a fourth: why were the scissors, which brought the murder unquestionably home to Harpenden, hidden where they were?'

God, I was being corny. Colombo didn't come within an ace of me! But, corny as it was, it got their attention. They goggled at me, in painful thought.

'Just like the party games we used to play when I

was a gel,' said Sybilla. 'I used to love brain-teasers.'

'I give up,' said Kate. 'Tell us the answers!'

'Right. Take the second of the questions first. Now, if I was going to kill my father while he was at his damned strappado, I think I'd try to give at least the appearance that the cord was worn away naturally. That was not done. Again, if I was going to cut the cord, I think I'd have used a sharp kitchen knife. That was not done either. Scissors were used. And consider at what height they were used. Where, if I was standing watching my father playing his silly and dangerous games, *where* would it be natural to snip the cord?'

I pantomimed a pair of scissors in my hand, and holding them at a natural height I snipped the air with them.

'How high was that? Over three feet from the ground, definitely. Very well, I'm tall. You, Mordred: you're about five feet nine. Where does it come natural to you to cut? . . . Well above two and a half feet from the ground, if I'm any judge.'

'Damned mathematics,' said Pete.

'But there's a point to it. The cord was snipped at little more than *two* feet from the floor.'

'For Christ's sake, he could have bloody bent down,' said Pete.

'Why should he? But that's what most of us here would have to have done.'

Maria-Luisa once again started up one of her train-whistle imprecations, and began going on about *bambini*. I held up my copper's hand for silence.

'You're getting the wrong end of the stick. Now, remember my third point: the light wasn't switched off. But surely it would have been natural for the murderer to try to cover up what was happening in some way: here was my father being slowly strappadoed to death, and yet his shadow could surely have been seen, through the curtains, from the grounds. Anyone might have come in and cut him down. And yet the light wasn't switched off.'

I heard Aunt Sybilla, under her breath, mutter 'A

167

Squealy', and Maria-Luisa shot a look like a stiletto in her direction.

'A Squealy, you say, Aunt Sybilla? But if it was a Squealy, wouldn't he (or she) either have just dropped the scissors on the floor and run? Or – if he was cunning – taken them back to the bathroom cupboard they came from? Hiding them argues *first* a knowledge of the enormity of the act, which I don't think any of the Squealies would have had; and *second* some knowledge that forensic science could have connected those scissors to the murder – and that they certainly wouldn't have had. Again, why did the murderer not get rid of the scissors outside the house? *Somewhere* in those enormous grounds. To slip out and chuck them in the lake would have been a natural impulse, even if we might eventually have found them, by dragging. And yet, they were hidden in the house, on the very floor the murder was committed on.'

Someone shifted uneasily. I thought it was Mordred. I was getting through. I went on quickly.

'It was when I put all those four things together that I realized that there was an alternative reading of the things that puzzled me. One that could be equally valid. I had concentrated on the theatricality of the whole set-up, the blatant self-advertisement. I had thought it – if you'll pardon me – typical of the family. But what if it was quite fortuitous? What if the murder was done like that because *there was no other way for the murderer to do it*?'

The silence was total. I had them in my hand, and as I looked at them I thought I saw dawning, reluctant understanding in one or two faces.

'Or to put it like this,' I went on, my voice rising with a touch of melodrama, of the old Trethowan theatricality: 'who *could* not have shot, knifed, poisoned, smothered anyone in what we may call the normal way, nor arranged a deceptive-looking accident? Who *could* not switch off the light, nor get out of the house to hide the scissors? Who would *naturally* have cut the cord of the machine at about two feet from the ground?'

I let my voice ring into silence. And in that silence Mordred looked at Uncle Lawrence. And Sybilla looked at Mordred, and then at Uncle Lawrence. And then the rest took their eyes off me, and looked at Uncle Lawrence. Lawrence himself seemed to have shrunk down into his rug. Suddenly the silence was broken.

'Oh, Lawrence,' giggled Kate. 'You didn't, did you? You are *naughty*!'

Lawrence – all eyes on him, thirsty for sensation – suddenly seemed to lose his passivity. He forced himself out of his rug and forward in his chair; he fixed me with a malevolent eye and began to raise his right arm. His quivering finger pointed at me, and he bellowed:

'You – you – damned—' but his arm refused to go higher, and he looked at it in horror – 'liar! AAAAAHHHH.'

The shriek was hideous, like a stuck pig, and the arm, which had seemed paralysed, clutched his heart as he let out breathless, agonized yelps, choking, spluttering, going hideously purple, like *The Death of Chatterton*.

'Oh, Perry,' howled Kate, genuinely concerned. 'Look what you've done. He's had a stroke.'

But before she could get to him, Tim was through the oak door, his men following, and he had Lawrence down on the floor, applying artificial respiration. Providentially – or rather, at my suggestion – they had a stretcher ready, and an ambulance outside. Within minutes, and still hard at the first aid, they were trundling him out of the room and pushing him head first into the ambulance at the door. I had stood aside while all this was going on, as if in unconcern. In fact, I (at least) was breathing normally, for the first time for half an hour. The plan had worked. I was going to be safe.

I was conscious, as the sound of the ambulance faded down the drive and along the road to Thornwick, that everybody was looking at me, and hardly in a spirit of friendship.

'That,' said Pete, 'was too bloody thick for words.'

'Was it?' I said. 'When we had come to that conclusion,

169

he would have had to be faced with it. If it had been done tête-à-tête, him and Hamnet, I imagine the result would have been the same.'

'You mean that he would have had a stroke?' asked Sybilla.

'I mean there would have been an appearance of that,' I said.

There was a long, long silence, as everybody tried to take in the significance of that. As for Lawrence as murderer, they all accepted it without difficulty: I suspected, with no evidence for my suspicion, that for many of them it was not too great a surprise. Who could tell what these odd people knew about each other, but preferred to conceal? Perhaps some of them were glad it was not someone nearer and dearer. Lawrence was hardly adept at making himself loved. But then, which of them was? Sybilla seemed to take the first word by some order of precedence.

'Poor, poor dear Lawrence,' she breathed, in a spirit of benediction. 'So it was Lawrence after all.'

'I'm afraid so,' I said. 'Lawrence couldn't switch off the light, because, as you all know, he could barely raise his hands as far as his mouth. He could manoeuvre his chair around the ground floor of the house, and around Kate's wing, which had the lift, but he couldn't go upstairs to the rest of the house, or into the garden. Scissors were much easier for a half-paralysed man to manage than a knife — he would have had to hold the cord in one hand and cut with the other: I doubt if he had the coordination, and it would have taken too much time. I said earlier there were perhaps other children in the house, besides the Squealies. Let's be charitable and assume that Lawrence did this when he was not in full control of his faculties. As far as the outside world is concerned, he did it in a fit of senile malice.'

'He wasn't so jolly senile,' said Aunt Kate.

'Don't be foolish, Kate,' said Sybilla sharply.

'As I say, we have to take the line that he was, whatever our suspicions, and whatever we feel about the supposed

170

stroke we have just witnessed. Uncle Lawrence will by now be in hospital. After that he will no doubt be put into some kind of institution, and the police doctors and psychiatrists will get on to him. I suspect that nobody will actually *want* to put him on trial. Who knows? Perhaps he *will* retreat into that other, shadow world of his.'

'Poor old man,' said Jan.

'Is that the end of the story, Daddy?' piped up an unregarded Daniel.

'Well, no,' I said. 'Not quite.'

'The *motive*,' said Mordred. 'If it wasn't a senile fit – and of course I don't believe that for a moment – then *why* did he do it?'

'Look here, Perry,' said Peter, stirring his flabby bulk uneasily. 'I get your point. My old dad did it, and I'm not denying it. Had half a suspicion that might be the case. Can't we leave it at that?'

'Not quite,' I said. 'You're trying to avoid *why* he did it. I think I know why you're trying to avoid it – I think it's because, by means we need not go into, you actually know. But if we leave it at that, you're all going to be asking questions for the rest of your lives. Was it some senile grudge of no importance, or was there something behind it? And if there was something behind it, are the rest of us safe? So I think you ought to know that there *was* something behind it: whether or not the killing was done when he was in his right mind, he had a motive. And at this point I'm going to have to ask you, *all* of you, to swear to keep what I'm about to tell you to yourselves. It's to be regarded as absolutely and permanently secret. Do you all swear to that?'

They all nodded their heads enthusiastically, greedily. Peter, I thought, nodded more enthusiastically and greedily than the rest. He realized I had no desire to rob him of his little kingdom.

'Then, if you all agree that what is coming goes no further than this room, I'll tell you. My mother, in the last years of her life, was on a cruise—'

171

'Oh, Perry,' howled Chris. 'You've found out. Do you have to tell everyone?'

'My sister,' I said, in my most elder-brotherly kind of way, 'who has not been as frank and open with me during this case as I should have liked, already knows what I'm about to tell you. Yes, Chris, I do have to tell them. This is murder, and if I don't, suspicion and distrust will go on festering for the rest of your lives. And apart from that, telling them is a form of protection for *you*. Right, then. My mother, on the round-the-world cruise she took in nineteen fifty-seven, met a woman who claimed to be, and undoubtedly was, the first Mrs Lawrence Trethowan.'

'Peregrine!' shrilled Sybilla. 'You don't mean it! Not the appalling Florrie! The Gibson girl!'

She looked around her in theatrical amazement. Pete looked furious; the rest were still taking it in.

'Jolly pretty little thing, wasn't she?' said Kate.

'I think she had worked in the theatre,' I said diplomatically. 'When my mother met her she owned or ran a hat shop in Sydney. The vital point, as you must all see, is that she was still alive in the 'fifties, not dead in the 'thirties as Lawrence had given out. And he had given it out, of course, because he was unable to divorce her. As perhaps you know, she was a Catholic. If she gave him no cause, and if she refused to divorce *him*, the marriage was virtually indissoluble. He was still legally married to her, as my mother realized, and for all I know he still may be. His second marriage was bigamous.'

'Oh, I say,' said Morrie, 'but that means—'

'You don't have to spell it out, for Christ's sake,' said Peter.

'No, let's not spell it out. But that's the reason why we all must keep it secret. Anyway, the rest can be told fairly quickly. My mother communicated this to me in a letter, to be sent to me on my twenty-first birthday. It was no doubt sent here by her lawyers, and appropriated by my father. I have no doubt it put him in a terrible quandary. On the one hand it made him Lawrence's legal heir, under the terms of Great-Grandfather's entail. On the other hand, he could not reasonably expect to enjoy the exalted position of head of the Trethowan family for long. Then it would inevitably descend to me. That he could not bear the thought of. He hated, absolutely hated me. I realize that now. So he compromised by screwing money out of Lawrence. He had been doing this, I imagine, since nineteen sixty-nine, the year I became twenty-one.'

'Ah – hence the stinginess!' said Kate.

'Precisely. Lawrence wanted to leave the estate as intact as possible to Peter, and via Peter to the eldest of the Squealies, whom he loved.'

'They have names!' said Maria-Luisa, suddenly, in English.

'Quite right. I beg your pardon. To . . . Pietro, is it? Mario? Pietro, yes. Lawrence did not dare to make over the estate to Peter in his lifetime, in case it aroused questions about the death of his first wife. That's why he'd gone to great lengths to keep his second divorce quiet and scandal-free. And all the time my father was slowly – not outrageously, but surely – milking him of money. And Lawrence knew that after he died, Peter would be milked in the same way. That wasn't the only drain on the estate: over the past few years his son had been filching pictures from the house and selling them off.'

'Come off it, Perry,' said Peter, with a cunning expression on his face. 'That was done with his consent. To keep paying off *your* damned father.'

'It's possible,' I said. 'Plausible. Perhaps we can leave it at that. We could prove it one way or the other by getting an expert to look at the signature on the authorization to sell which you gave to the Newstead Abbey people. Shall we do that? No? Well, personally I suspect that he did not authorize that or any other sale, but he did consent to cover up for you afterwards. That, as I said, is a minor matter. What does seem to be clear is that my father, in the last few weeks, began to make his demands more pressing. Why? Well, I don't know, but I wonder whether it wasn't just for fun. Just as the tortures got more and more extreme, so Lawrence had to wriggle more, otherwise my papa didn't get his kick. And Lawrence took the necessary steps and killed him in the only way he could think of. He simulated an "off-day"—'

'I said he was often spoofing,' said Kate.

'—got out from Kate's wing in the lift, got easily over to the Gothic wing, used the scissors he had secreted earlier, hid them *also* on the ground floor, near the wing which had no connection with him or his, and went back to Kate's.'

'Doesn't sound as if he was having a senile fit to me,' said Kate.

'As far as we are concerned, that is the explanation we must press,' I said patiently. 'Ultimately it will be up to the police doctors, and the psychiatrists. If Uncle Lawrence is the man I take him for, he will make mince-meat of the psychiatrists. I would think it in the highest degree unlikely that he will ever come to trial. What is important is that we all, now we have heard the truth, put it *absolutely* out of our minds. I need hardly say I have no intention of acting on this information. Everything will remain as it was, and Pete will take over when Lawrence dies — or, as I suspect, rather before.' I looked round at him. Peter was expressing no great gratitude, but he did look relieved. 'Well, that's all I have to say. I'm sorry it took so long. Now I need a drink, and I expect you do too.'

I drew my fist across my forehead. It was wet as hell, and my clean shirt was nastily damp. But all that mattered was that I had got through it. I had managed it. Lawrence was on his way to some kind of clink, and I was out of the wood. Soon Jan and Daniel and I would be out of the snake-pit and on our way to Newcastle.

But then suddenly things took a terrible turn. So far, I had been in control, immaculately in control. Now the situation developed an impetus, took a direction, which was none of my choosing. The end of the nightmare had been in sight: suddenly the scenario changed and a totally new nightmare took over, of terrifying dimensions.

'Hold!' said Sybilla.

Sybilla must be the only person in the world today who can say 'Hold!' and not mean to get a laugh. I was on my way to the drinks tray, but I stopped in my tracks. Was she begrudging me a glass of their lousy sherry?

'Perry, my dear boy,' said Sybilla, fluttering a bit of magenta drape in my direction. 'I know I speak for all of us when I say we understand and appreciate the *nobility* of your gesture of renunciation. The generosity and selflessness of it staggers one, simply takes away the breath! It is a gesture in the true Trethowan tradition. But it will not do, dear boy!'

'Aunt Sybilla, it is not a selfless—'

'It simply will not do! I know that in what I am about to say I speak for Kate—'

'Oh, rather!' said Kate. 'For once!'

'—and naturally Mordred will agree with me too. I know I speak for them when I say that right must be done. Grandfather Josiah's intentions were made perfectly plain: the house and the associated properties, shares and money went to the *legitimate* heir in the *male* line. (His view of women was regrettable, but of its time.) His feelings, were he to find out that the house and the *large* sums of money and land that go with it had descended to someone born on the wrong side of the blanket, are not to be thought of. He was brought up a Presbyterian! The moral standards required of his domestic servants were strict even for those times. I can only say that for all of us, you, Perry – on Lawrence's demise, or incapacity, which, as you say, seems only too likely – will be, *must* be, head of the family.'

'You're pretty quick to give away my property,' said Peter resentfully.

'I should have thought it would be clear even to one of your intellectual capacity that one thing the property is not, is yours,' said Sybilla, with more than her usual asperity.

'Aunt Sybilla!' cried Cristobel. 'Peter has *always* been brought up to regard himself as heir.' She was rewarded by a look of venomous suspicion from Maria-Luisa.

'Then he should have *acted* as such,' said Sybilla. 'Peter has *never* been committed to the family, as a family. I fear that Peter has never been committed to anyone but himself. Hard words, especially of a Trethowan, but how true! I know that Kate and I and Mordred have been *fearful* of our future, when Lawrence should pass on. Our very living here might have been threatened! He might have demanded rent! It is quite clear that we owe no loyalty to Peter.'

'Pete's a robber,' said Kate.

'Indeed, if I understand you right, Peregrine, Peter has in fact *known* of this for some time, and kept it quiet.'

'Yes,' I said. 'I think so. But—'

'How unworthy!' pronounced Sybilla, with dire finality. 'Now you, Perry — I can only say that as soon as you came into this room the other day, I marked you down as a man of real sensitivity. Of truly refined feeling. And of deep *family* feeling.'

I almost laughed out loud at the blatant mendacity of the woman. 'Aunt Sybilla,' I said. 'I think this conversation should be nipped in the bud straight away. I simply could never agree to take on the responsibilities that owning Harpenden would entail. I have no desire to. You forget that my commitment to the family is even less than Peter's. I have had nothing whatever to do with it for fourteen years.'

'That is quite irrelevant, my dear boy! The result of an unfortunate misunderstanding. One has only to look at you, standing here now, to sense in you the qualities of a Trethowan. I'm sure you, Jan dear, will bear me out that

176

Peregrine is, and thinks of himself as, a true Trethowan, and is proud of it!'

'Perry's always been very taken up with his family,' said Jan. 'He thinks of you a lot.'

The treachery of it! The blank treachery! I threw Jan a glance of impending thunder.

'There!' said Sybilla triumphantly. 'Nor, Peregrine, can you think only of yourself in this. There are the interests of your dear little boy to consider. It's unthinkable that he be deprived of what is undoubtedly his by right.' (At this point a squawk came from Maria-Luisa.) 'By right!' repeated Sybilla magisterially. 'You must think what is best for Daniel.'

'I do not think that inheriting large wads of money is necessarily the best thing that can happen to a man,' I said. 'Quite the reverse. Nor do I think I want Daniel saddled with a ridiculous white elephant of a house.'

It was the wrong thing to say altogether. 'I like it here,' said Daniel stoutly. 'I think it's scrumptious here!'

'Precisely,' said Sybilla. 'You would confine the poor child to a tiny little flat in – where is it?'

'Maida Vale.'

'Maida Vale. Goodness me, I remember it being built. It was where London businessmen kept their fancy women! And very suitable it was too, no doubt, for such a purpose. But it is hardly an ideal place for a growing child. When one thinks too of Jan, it is surely obvious what an eminently gracious *châtelaine* of Harpenden she would make. Your father, my dear, you said was—?'

'A house-painter,' said Jan.

Aunt Sybilla was unperturbed. 'I have always maintained that what the Trethowans needed was an infusion of working-class blood.'

'Uncle Lawrence did his best,' I said, 'but you didn't seem exactly delighted.'

Sybilla ignored me. 'Then surely we can regard it all as settled. We cannot allow you, as a result of a truly *quixotic* whim, or some *absurd* notion of chivalry, to

177

rob yourself and your lovely little boy of your rightful heritage.'

I drew my fingers round my shirt collar, and felt them wet from the sweat. This was coming altogether too close. 'This is truly nonsensical, Aunt Syb,' I said. 'I'm a working man, I love my job. I have no intention of giving it up to take over a useless fortune I haven't earned, and a monstrous house I've always loathed. I hope to do something a little more useful with my life.'

'Maintaining the heritage of the Trethowans is hardly useless,' said Sybilla. 'And it is a job you are eminently suited for. It has been clear to us, Perry, since you arrived, clear to Mordred, and to Kate, and to me—'

'You'd make a lovely head of the family,' said Kate. 'And fancy Jan's father being a house-painter!'

'As I was saying, Kate dear, we have watched you, Perry, since your return among us. We have seen you . . . *expand*! It is clear that your job, admirable and useful in its rather prosaic way, does not *stretch* your capacities.'

'I always understood you found my *size* horribly unspiritual,' I said.

'Let us not take amiss words spoken in the heat of the moment. I have in fact always had a *penchant* for large men. We must remember that Grandfather Josiah was himself a fine, large man.'

'I will not be compared to Great-Grandfather Josiah!' I shouted.

'It's true, Perry, you know,' said Jan, compounding her treachery. 'You have grown into the place. Just looking at you walking around the grounds, it seemed you belonged here.'

'He's certainly been acting as if he owned the place since he came, if that's what you mean,' said Pete resentfully.

'*And so he will*!' said Aunt Sybilla. 'Come, Peregrine, do tell us that my poor, feeble words have made you see sense.'

'No, Aunt Sybilla,' I said. 'Quite the reverse. Nothing on earth would induce me to take on the burden of

Harpenden. I shall return after the weekend to my poky little flat in Maida Vale, and when I bump my head on the low ceilings and bang my elbows into inconvenient cupboards I shall not for one moment regret not being the owner of Harpenden. Of course I shall hope to see you all often in the future—' (lies! lies!) '—but I fear I shall never under any circumstances become head of the family. The secret will remain a secret.'

But then the slippery Sybilla suddenly changed her tack. 'That, I'm afraid, is hardly possible.'

'You swore—'

'Oh, certainly. If one takes note of such things. The law certainly takes no cognizance of them. But what precisely have I sworn? Not to reveal that your mother, by coincidence, discovered the existence of the first Mrs Trethowan. No doubt I shall hold to my oath. But there are many more ways than one of coming at a fact such as that.'

'Clever old Syb!' said Kate.

'The date of Florence Trethowan's death can certainly be established by enquiry at Somerset House, or wherever they keep the records these days. No doubt Australia has an equivalent if that fails — I believe they have kept excellent records there since convict times. I shall write off tomorrow if you are obdurate. It may be, of course, that she is not dead, even now. Conceivably there is a Lady Trethowan in some Old People's establishment in Bondi, or Manley, the sleeping partner in a hat shop. That would be the best evidence of all. So you see, your mother is not the only possible witness to the irregularity of Peter's birth.'

'Why the hell do you go on about that?' Peter burst out. 'I thought the Trethowans were supposed to be so bloody unorthodox.'

'Unorthodox, maybe, but *never* illegitimate.' Chris looked at the floor, her face burning. 'Come, Perry, be sensible about this. Accept gracefully your *true* position! Do not have greatness *thrust* upon you!'

179

'Come on, Perry,' said Kate. 'I bet you've got a *lovely* seat on a horse! And you'd make a topping magistrate!'

'I do think you ought to give it a try, Perry,' said Jan. 'You've got to remember, it was only your father you disagreed with, not the whole family.'

'I do like it here,' said Dan, with the obstinate monotony of childhood. 'Would it all be mine?'

I stood there in anguished thought. Twisters, they'd got me. An oath meant nothing to an elderly snake like Sybilla who has a privileged position to defend. Even my own wife and son had crossed the picket lines to the other side. They had trapped me, beaten me on to the ropes. I thought of living here, day after day, month after month, year after year; thought of sitting nightly at the head of the table, listening to Sybilla's vinegarish asininities, enduring Kate's boisterous puppyishness, being the butt of Peter's sniping. I thought of Dan growing up with the Squealies. I thought of sitting on the bench, going to rural shows, mixing with the Northern gentry, who would remark behind my back that I was the son of that Trethowan who had been murdered while – had you heard? – guffaw . . .

But were their guffaws any worse than the manly guffaws of my colleagues at the Yard, their assertions of healthy normality? At least I wouldn't have to work every day with the Northumberland squirearchy. I thought of walking the grounds with Jan and Daniel; I thought of Daniel growing up with room to be free in, to wander and to explore at will; I thought of being rid of the slog and paperwork of life in the CID, of washing my hands of the petty crooks, wheedling for one more chance, of the big, sleek crooks trying to slip me a bribe, I thought of getting shot of all the sleaziness, the stench of evil, the vileness . . .

My agonized meditation was interrupted by McWatters. Entering hurriedly, he walked straight over to me (showing that he had been listening at the door). He looked unaccustomedly confused and worried.

'Mr Peregrine, sir. There's someone arrived. A . . . gentleman . . .'

'Well?'

'He says he's Mr Wallace Trethowan.'

'Who?'

'Mr Wallace, sir. Elder son of Sir Lawrence.'

And there entered unannounced into the drawing-room a large brown man of around sixty, with a broad-brimmed hat, cavalry-twill trousers and chukka-boots, followed by an encouraging-sized family.

'Greetings, all,' he said, in broad Australian. 'Thought we'd drop in as we were passing. Old place looks smaller than it used to. Jeez, it's nice to be back, though. Anyone going to offer me a nice cool beer?'

CHAPTER 16

EPILOGUE

You lot were expecting that all along, I suppose. For you this has just been a book, and in books people who are 'missing, presumed dead' always turn up by the end. For me, this was all for real, and I'd been used all my life to looking on Cousin Wallace as dead. If Wallace was not dead, indeed, I owed my very existence to a bureaucratic error.

We got the whole story, at boozy length, over the next few days. Wallace had gone with his mother to Australia in 1933. His father had never shown any great interest in him, beyond inviting him a couple of times to Harpenden, where he had been rather grandly neglected (this, remember, was the time when the Trethowans' artistic pretensions were at their height). When they left these shores, all contact between them and the English Trethowans had ceased. On the outbreak of war, Wallace (or Wally as he insisted we call him) had come back to Europe, enlisted, and found himself in a Guards regiment. It did not take him long to be 'really pissed off, if you'll pardon the expression' with the bull, the snobbery, the grind and the danger. And so in 1944, during the Arnhem action, he just 'took off', which was his nice way of saying he deserted. He made his way, somehow, through the chaos of Central Europe at that time, through countries emerging out of one ghastly tyranny, and about to fall victim to another. In the end he made it to Greece, where he got a job on a cargo boat which finally took him back to Australia.

He seems never to have joined up with his mother again ('she lived her own life, and between you and I she was a bit of an embarrassment'), but eventually he worked his way up to owning an enormous property in outback Queensland: thousands of square miles, thousands of head of cattle, and hardly enough water to bathe a baby in. Only a man with a property like that could conceivably find Harpenden smaller than he remembered it. This was the family's first trip back to the Old Country.

I don't for a moment believe that their turning up at Harpenden was entirely coincidental. They said they were on their way to Scotland in the Land-Rover, which was no doubt true enough. But I suspect they had read about our little troubles in one of the sensational rags Sybilla had been feeding information to, had been intrigued, and had started wondering about poor old Lawrence, and what pickings there might be for them when he died.

They certainly got more than they bargained for. Uncle Lawrence, as I foresaw, totally deceived the examining psychiatrists (there is no one, but no one, more gullible than a psychiatrist), very much as I believe he had been deceiving his family in the year since his stroke: I think most of his 'off-days' were assumed, were a preparation for the murder which he finally so ingeniously accomplished. But three months later he died of a second stroke, while declaiming his poetry to the other inmates of the institution he had been confined to. He died as he lived, a grandiose old phoney, and the Wallace Trethowans were now masters of Harpenden.

It didn't go well. It was an exceptionally cold winter, Harpenden is impossible to heat at the best of times, Aunt Sybilla got on their nerves, and the McWatterses, finding that the tone of the place had gone down, left for more prestigious employ. I met Wally in London for lunch one day, and when I'd listened (with the most genuine sympathy) to his beefing for half an hour, I

183

suggested he made the house over to the country, or to the National Trust, and hotfoot it back to Australia with what remained of the loot. It wasn't easy to manage, the financial climate of the country being what it is, but finally it went through. Harpenden House became a museum of nineteenth- and twentieth-century arts, subject to the present residents having the right to remain in their living quarters.

It works very nicely. Aunt Syb shows people round, descants on the Friths and the Holman Hunts and the Luke Fildeses, and most people imagine she dates from the same era as the pictures. When she comes to the Elizabeth Trethowan Gallery, which is housed in the Elizabethan wing, she draws attention to what she calls the 'tiny little faults' in the work of her sister, which she says 'only the eye of a fellow artist' can detect. There has even been a slight revival of interest in Aunt Kate: little parties of National Front supporters come to see her Collection, and though after the first such visit she remarked wistfully that they were not quite the superb specimens of Aryan youth she had been expecting, by now her romantic mind has managed to create a halo of the heroic even around them.

Pete vacated the Elizabethan wing very shortly after Wally took over. He had developed a close working relationship with the director of the Museum of Women's Art in Philadelphia, and he decamped to the States to make it still closer. He took three of Eliza's pictures, to ensure a warm welcome. Maria-Luisa and the Squealies took themselves back to Naples, where Maria-Luisa assumed a position of some power and influence in a branch of the Mafia her family was involved with. The Squealies are considered fine children in the Italian South, but Aunt Sybilla has been heard to remark, almost hopefully, on the high incidence of fatal childish diseases in the Naples area. Cristobel had her baby, and is the better for it, and I hope it is having a happier childhood in the Gothic wing than ever Chris and I had. Jan and I had a postcard, all lakes and scrubland, from Mordred the other day. He is with the British Council in Finland, where no doubt he is learning more enchanting things to do with herrings.

As you can imagine, Jan and I had a few bad days after the spectacular treachery of her joining Sybilla's eleven to play against me. I roughed her up a bit, verbally, and she pretended it had all been a joke, to see how I took it. After a time I said that I believed her. On the scaffold of such mutual deceptions is the stability of married life built. She has just done well in her second-year exams at Newcastle, and is beginning to wonder what to do with a degree in Arabic.

Well, so now you've heard the story of how I shopped my uncle for murdering my dad, caught the bastard cousin pinching the family pictures, discovered my sister was pregnant by the same bastard cousin, and all the rest of the little oddities and secrets of one of the grand old families that make this country what it is today. The whole thing was sheer torture from beginning to end, and if I confess that I enjoyed it now and then, you will say, I suppose, that that, at least, I got from my father. Now it's all out in the open, though, couldn't we call it a day? You can put it out of your mind, and I can go on with my life. I do have a job of work to do.

THE END

POLITICAL SUICIDE
by Robert Barnard

When the MP for Bootham East was fished out of the Thames it looked like a clear case of suicide. But as Superintendent Sutcliffe's investigations got under way, and as the by-election for his successor hotted up, some very murky political waters were stirred up. The local Labour party had been hijacked by the extreme left, the Tory Party had a most unpleasant young candidate (apart from being inarticulate) had something nasty in his past he would prefer to forget. In fact, by the time polling day came it was very obvious that the political suicide was no suicide, but murder.

'Sharp-edged, witty, and politically spot-on,' *The Times*

'Bitterly, bitingly funny,' *Scotsman*

'One of the funniest men writing mysteries today'
Washington Post

'A wickedly funny hatchet job on the mother of parliaments'
Observer

'As usual, with all the votes in, Barnard wins, hands down,
Sunday Times

'What makes this a star turn is Barnard's sharp, often hilarious picture of the hustings. An irresistible party piece.'
Guardian

0 552 13128 8

DISPOSAL OF THE LIVING
by Robert Barnard

'Sharp, sly and funny portrait of local rivalries and obsessions confirming Barnard as one of our most original and versatile blood-spillers.'
The Times

'A pacy, entertaining read, with plenty of chuckles and cunning plotting'
Police

'Smart updating of village mystery, with Mr B. displaying a wonderful eye and ear for snobbery, malice, and other small-town delights'
Scotsman

'One of the wittiest comedies of manners'
Punch

When the women of Hexton-upon-Weir decided to band together to block the appointment of a new vicar who was not only unacceptably High Church but also – oh horror! – celibate, they managed to create merry hell. As the town was riven by faction and counter-faction, Helen Kitterege, wife of the local vet, tried to remain aloof, but finally, during the town's fete, the ill-will and plotting degenerated into murder, a murder that affected Helen more than anyone else. Somewhere among the secrets of this female dominated town was a key shame that someone was prepared to kill for.

0 552 13129 6

OUT OF THE BLACKOUT
by Robert Barnard

'Mr Barnard unswathes his riddle with great skill. I suspect he is going to outwit all but a handful of his readers'
New York Times

'We can be sure of an original plot from Robert Barnard, one of the best in the field'
Police

'The chameleon talent of Mr Barnard has once again taken colouration from a background of dreadful vibrancy'
Sunday Times

'Barnard's invention is unflagging: the book is a real achievement'
Financial Times

In 1941, at the height of the Blitz, a trainload of children, evacuees, arrived at the West Country station of Yeasdon. And when they were counted there was one evacuee too many. Simon Thorn, about five years old, small, exhausted, could not be traced back to his home in London, and could remember almost nothing of his background. The only link with the past was his recurring nightmare – of a murder. It was many years before Simon went back to London, went back to an eerie house in Paddington that filled him with dread and to the unravelling of a vicious crime that had never been detected.

0 552 13127 X

BODIES
by Robert Barnard

'What an ear Robert Barnard has! In his new novel set in the sleazy world of body-building and the adjacent world of soft porn, he gets the language just right'
Financial Times

Bodies was a mild and rather innocuous 'naughty' magazine, and really rather respectable in a seedy and run-down sort of way. The morning he opened the door of his solo photographic studio and found the place plastered with bodies – dead bodies – was more than he could cope with. Perry Trethowan of Scotland Yard found him in a state of hysterical collapse.

As Perry began to dig into the world of muscle-men, photographers, and models, he discovered that behind the beautiful bodies lurked some very unpleasant secrets – one of which had culminated in the mass Soho slaughter.

'He plots a mystery as well as any other writer alive. And he never takes the easy path of repeating a winning formula.'
Time Magazine

0 552 13237 3

COMING SOON
A CORPSE IN A GILDED CAGE
by Robert Barnard

'A delectably risible tale with ample surprises as well as social barbs and a crowning reversal for traditionalists'
Guardian

Chetton Hall was one of Britain's noblest and stateliest of stately piles. The Spenders had lived in Chetton since 1610, amassing treasures, wealth, and several layers of dignity and pomp. Which made it all the more shocking when Percy Spender of Clapham ascended to the title. There was no denying that the new Earl was 'not quite' and his ghastly family were not at all. When they all descended on Chetton Hall on Percy's sixtieth birthday their main desire was to see just what Percy was going to do with his new-found wealth, and what was in it for them.

But as the jolly house party got under way something most unpleasant occurred. For in the niche by the stairwell, lying beside the famous Bernini marble, a body was discovered. Killed by a karate blow to the neck. And it was fairly obvious that one of the new Earl's family had done it.

'Mr Barnard is always good with noble eccentricity. The smart throwaway lines, the sharp character vignettes, the ironic asides do not obstruct the unfolding of a well-made plausible story'
William Weaver, Financial Times

0 552 13368 X

A SELECTED LIST OF CRIME TITLES AVAILABLE FROM CORGI BOOKS

☐ 12792 2	**THE COMPLETE STEEL**	*Catherine Aird*	£2.50
☐ 12793 0	**HENRIETTA WHO?**	*Catherine Aird*	£2.50
☐ 12794 9	**A LATE PHOENIX**	*Catherine Aird*	£1.95
☐ 13426 0	**PARTING BREATH**	*Catherine Aird*	£2.50
☐ 13237 3	**BODIES**	*Robert Barnard*	£2.50
☐ 13129 6	**THE DISPOSAL OF THE LIVING**	*Robert Barnard*	£2.50
☐ 13127 X	**OUT OF THE BLACKOUT**	*Robert Barnard*	£2.50
☐ 13128 8	**POLITICAL SUICIDE**	*Robert Barnard*	£2.50
☐ 12804 X	**WYCLIFFE AND THE PEA GREEN BOAT**	*W. J. Burley*	£2.50
☐ 12806 6	**WYCLIFFE AND THE SCAPEGOAT**	*W. J. Burley*	£2.50
☐ 13232 2	**WYCLIFFE AND THE BEALES**	*W. J. Burley*	£2.50
☐ 13231 4	**WYCLIFFE AND THE FOUR JACKS**	*W. J. Burley*	£2.50
☐ 13235 7	**MALICE DOMESTIC**	*Mollie Hardwick*	£2.50
☐ 13292 6	**THE QUEEN'S HEAD**	*Edward Marston*	£2.99
☐ 12021 9	**RUMPELSTILTSKIN**	*Ed McBain*	£1.50
☐ 13240 3	**A HELL OF A WOMAN**	*Jim Thompson*	£2.50
☐ 13239 X	**THE KILL OFF**	*Jim Thompson*	£2.50
☐ 13242 X	**RECOIL**	*Jim Thompson*	£2.50
☐ 13256 X	**SAVAGE NIGHT**	*Jim Thompson*	£2.50